PSYCHOTIC EPISODES

for Fionnuala

and

The Talking Stick

Alan McMonagle

PSYCHOTIC EPISODES

ARLEN
HOUSE

PSYCHOTIC EPISODES

is published in 2013 by
ARLEN HOUSE
42 Grange Abbey Road
Baldoyle
Dublin 13
Ireland
Phone/Fax: 353 86 8207617
Email: arlenhouse@gmail.com

Distributed internationally by
SYRACUSE UNIVERSITY PRESS
621 Skytop Road, Suite 110
Syracuse, NY 13244–5290
Phone: 315–443–5534/Fax: 315–443–5545
Email: supress@syr.edu

978–1–85132–053–0, paperback
978–1–85132–063–9, hardback

Typesetting by Arlen House
Printing by Brunswick Press
Front Cover Collage by Aoife Casby is entitled 'Pericope 4'
Back Cover Image by Aoife Casby is entitled 'But Once Visible'
www.aoifecasby.net

Psychotic Episodes has received
financial assistance from the Arts
Council under the Publications/
Title by Title Scheme

CONTENTS

ACKNOWLEDGEMENTS

'Psychotic Episodes' was published in *Grain* (Canada) and nominated for a 2011 Pushcart Prize.

'Looking After Little Patrick' was published in *The Adirondack Review* (USA).

'The Storyteller and the Thief' was shortlisted for the 2011 William Trevor/Elizabeth Bowen short story prize and was published in *Prairie Fire* (Canada).

'Women Drivers on Taylor's Hill' was shortlisted for the 2012 Fish Short Story Prize and appears in the anthology *Galway Stories* (Doire Press, 2013).

'Bleeding Boy' was chosen by Kevin Barry for the 'Lonely Voice' reading series at the Irish Writers' Centre.

'The Night My Sister Almost Fixed Me Up With a Porn Star' appeared in *Crannóg*.

'The Good Crank' was published in *Motif* (USA).

'Beside Titan's Sea' was the 2011 winner of the Writing Spirit Award (judge: Christine Dwyer Hickey) and was published in *Natural Bridge* (USA).

'Walking Among Ruins in Babylon' was published in *The Valparaiso Fiction Review* (USA).

'Runaways' was a runner-up in the 2012 *RTÉ Guide*/Penguin Ireland short story competition and shortlisted for the 2012 Molly Keane short story award.

'The Fortune Teller and the Rebel' was published in *Mentor* (Slovenia).

'Bloomsday Bus Driver' appeared in *The Galway Review*.

'Untouchable' was published in *The Irish Times*.

PSYCHOTIC EPISODES

LOOKING AFTER LITTLE PATRICK

The child next door to us is always crying. We think up ways of dealing with it. Silver bullets. A stake through the heart. Exorcism. Hours later, Gemma sighs and wonders why his parents allow him make so much noise. As a last resort, I mention some Japanese methods I recall reading about in a faraway museum. In our house, it's just the two of us and, perhaps, that's just as well.

Once, before our doctor ruled it out as a possibility, Gemma and I spoke about making a baby. We decided on a boy and gave him a fully formed personality. He had a quiet intensity and large arms. He had a wonderful ability to say the same thing over and over again without sounding repetitive. He didn't need things to be explained to him more than once. We called him Marlon after our favourite actor. If he wanted to join us in a glass of wine at mealtime we said that was OK. During our meal, the child next door started crying again and we told Marlon he must never do that. The crying continued and Gemma and I shook our fists at the wall separating us from our neighbours. Marlon could wait, we decided.

Today – a clear though breezy early winter Sunday – we have volunteered to look after Gemma's nephew. He is known as Little Patrick. He is five years old, and enjoys climbing and starring in home movies. From previous child-minding adventures we know it is a mistake offering to look after him, but Gemma likes to do a good deed now and again. Little Patrick's parents – Gemma's brother, Joe, and his wife, Audrey – have a wedding to attend, and their regular child-sitter is temporarily refusing any contact with Little Patrick after he flushed her new earrings down the toilet. They were a gift from her boyfriend.

'Of course we will look after Little Patrick', we say when the call comes through. 'Send him in on the train'.

'He's five years old', his mother reminds us.

'Well make sure they don't charge him full whack', we say.

Instead of by train, Little Patrick arrives in his father's large car. He arrives with a tractor and trailer, a DVD called *Shark Tale*, a story book called *Abdul, Susie and the Lollipop*, a change of clothes and a CD of Johnny Cash's greatest hits.

'Would you like a cocktail?' I ask him, as soon as his father has left. 'I make a really good Long Island Iced Tea'.

He doesn't say anything to this, instead climbs onto the high chair at our breakfast bar and stares at me. I take this as a Yes and get busy with the blender.

'Who is that silly man making a mess?' Gemma asks Little Patrick as I slosh around my cocktail shaker, spilling lemon juice and fizzing cola everywhere. Again, he doesn't answer. He just keeps staring at me.

'He's a shy boy', says Gemma, patting him on the head.

'He's a bit like our little guy', I say, pouring tumblers of the cocktail. 'He has a quiet intensity'.

This all changes as soon as he sees the tumblers of Long Island Iced Tea I have prepared. Quickly, he drinks three and I drink two. I am tempted to pour some Bacardi into his fourth. He can't get enough of them into him. When he becomes hyperactive and emotional Gemma decides we should go to the beach. She grabs her camera, I buckle Little Patrick into the back seat of our car and off we go.

We drive to the beach, find a parking space along the promenade in front of the water, and turn to Little Patrick to make sure he is still excited. As we assist him out of his seat, we close the car door on his thumb. At once, I re-open the car door, release the trapped thumb and pretend no harm has been done. Gemma fusses over Little Patrick's wonderful coat, points to the waves caressing the strand below us and, for a moment, we think we will get away with it. However, he starts to cry. As he cries and cries, the thumb starts to turn black.

'It will fall off if you keep crying', I say to him, pointing at his scary thumb.

'We need a bandage', Gemma says and she clutches him to her, and takes turns to kiss his injury and say bad bold door to our innocent car.

'He is making a really annoying sound', I say.

'So would you if someone tried to take off *your* thumb', says Gemma.

'Let's throw him in the water'.

'Maybe we should skip the beach', says Gemma, when it is obvious that no amount of sand and sea is going to alleviate Little Patrick's distress.

We decide to drive into town. On our way, we stop by the woods. Gemma and I often walk together there on Sundays. It's where we have some of our best conversations. As well as children and marriage, we have talked about music, places we would like to see, the state of our parents' health, the economic downturn and Barack Obama.

Gemma loves talking about Barack. Any mention of him always seems to pep her up. He has a nice smile, she says. The assassin will remove that smile, I say. He is so charismatic, she says. Tell that to his undertaker, I say. He will fix the world, she says. I thought a woman was going to do that, I say.

Gemma says many more things about Barack. She reads everything about him in the newspapers too. And turns on the television whenever he is due to make one of his inspirational speeches. Barackitis I call it. So bad is her condition I had to order his book for her from Amazon and, then, bid outrageously on eBay for a *New York Times* the morning after he won the election.

When we finish this Sunday's conversation Little Patrick is nowhere to be seen. He has disappeared. At once and with both hands, Gemma starts pulling at her hair. I try to stay calm.

'Please tell me this isn't happening', Gemma says scanning the leafless trees all around us, her hands now clamped to either side of her head.

'This sort of thing happens all the time', I say.

'How are we going to find him among all these trees? He's very small. He might have fallen down a foxhole'.

'Maybe he's chasing that fox', I say, pointing to a fast-moving reddish thing upon the ridge ahead of us.

'I'm going to kill that fox', says Gemma, hurrying off.

As I watch her scurry onto the ridge, then fade inside the trees, I think of the time I disappeared. It was when I was little also, though perhaps not quite so little as Little Patrick. As a boy, I used to like hunting for horse chestnuts, and every autumn I threw my stick at the tree growing beyond the back garden of our house. One autumn, my father brought me to a forest along the edges of our town – at least I thought it was a forest, everything was so large back then. He threw his sticks at the tallest trees while I sought out one short enough to accept my feeble throws. I wandered away from my father and looked for a suitable tree. I remember drifting deep into the forest. As I wandered further and further among the trees I could hear my father calling out, but I ignored his calls and continued my search. Eventually, I happened upon a small clearing and, growing out of the ground at a skewed angle, was the tree I had been searching for. It was so skewed it looked as though it wanted to grow along the ground instead of taking its place amongst the others. 'Leave that one alone', I remember my father saying when he got to me. 'A tree born crooked will never grow straight'.

When we catch up to him, Little Patrick is standing on a tree stump, swinging a squirrel by its tail. I tell him we will cook the squirrel for dinner, but that first I have to check it for signs of ringworm. When he stops swinging the squirrel and presents it to me, I pretend I am afraid. Little Patrick starts laughing at my fear, and in the ensuing trepidation, the squirrel evades my nervous hands and scurries up a tree. Then Gemma clutches Little Patrick to her. He is still laughing when we get back to the car.

On our way into town, we stop at a pharmacy and purchase an elaborate bandage for the injured thumb. Further on again, we park near the open pier, where the river surges into the bay. It's our favourite part of town. Sometimes the tidewater is so high it laps over the pier walls. Other times, the river and sea waters are angry, and they clash mercilessly. Today, the waters have declared a temporary peace, the swans have made an appearance, and we take Little Patrick over to see them.

Some swans are bobbing on the water, resting. Others drift with the current. And one or two have waddled out of the water, up the boat ramp and onto the pier, and are accepting crumbs of bread tossed from un-needed loaf-wrappers. Little Patrick walks right up to one, and stares at the orange beak pinching the ground before him. He shoves his bandaged thumb up in the air just as Gemma takes a photograph.

We walk further along the pier. It juts right out into the bay and the further along it we walk the deeper the water becomes. Little Patrick likes keeping close to the edge in order that he may better see into the water. Mentally, I prepare myself for when Little Patrick disappears again, and I must plunge into the deepening water to search for his little body. Gemma takes more photographs.

At the end of the pier a spiky breeze is blowing in off the open water. An old man and his dog stand at the edge of the pier. Two fishermen cast their lines and hope for the best. I notice that they have already caught something and thrown it in a bucket placed on the wall raised along the windward end of the pier.

'What did you get?' I ask them.

'A flounder', one of them replies, the younger one.

I point out the bucket to Little Patrick. 'Look, a flounder', I say, and he saunters over to inspect it.

'Do you think we should get a dog?' I ask Gemma, turning my attention to the old man who has knelt down to pat the shaggy-looking thing at his heel.

'Before he moves in to the White House, Barack is going to buy his little girls a puppy', Gemma says. 'He's hoping to get one from a shelter. A mutt, he says. Maybe, we could do that'.

'He sounds like the right man for the job', I say.

'He is the only man for the job', says Gemma.

'You do know he can't count', I say. 'He thinks there are fifty-seven states in America. I suppose there are if you include Ireland and England, and a few other places. But I don't think he was thinking along those lines'.

'He gives great answers', Gemma says.

'All he says is "Yes we can"'.

'That's a great answer'.

When we turn to him, Little Patrick is up on the wall. There is no barrier. Just a thirty-foot drop into the water below, which Little Patrick will know about if he runs for a couple of more steps.

'Oh Jesus!' Gemma says and freezes to the spot where she is standing. I launch myself, and manage to wrap my hand around one of his busy legs, and haul him from the wall. At once, Gemma takes him from me, and sits down with her back to the wall, holding Little Patrick. She clutches him close to her, rocks him gently, and they sit like that together until long after the fishermen catch another fish and the old man has disappeared. I stand there watching them together and wonder why relatives ask us to look after their children. At some point I grab the camera and take some photographs of Gemma with Little Patrick. They look cosy together and a pang of disappointment flutters through me.

Eventually, we gather ourselves, and go for a Pizza. I order a Sloppy Giuseppe, Gemma goes for something with pineapple, and Little Patrick contents himself with toppings of Chef brown sauce, Heinz ketchup and Hellmann's mayonnaise. In no time his head resembles a large multi-coloured lollipop. Gemma takes another photograph. Then we bring him back to our house.

Back at the house, Gemma transfers her photographs from her camera to the computer. She has a file called *my pictures* and in it she keeps photographs of our child-minding adventures. She has one of her two-year-old niece, Saoirse, who has no hair and looks terrified, possibly because kneeling towards her is a green-faced man with a set of Dracula fangs protruding from his mouth. There is one of her three-year-old nephew, Paulito, who divides his time between Portugal and Ireland, and can speak three languages. He has a great mop of curly hair and doesn't look too happy, possibly because he is sitting in the black vinyl chair at my local barber shop about to have his curls cut off. Then there is one of my eight-year-old nephew, Cian. He is holding up a drawing of a burning-down house which, if memory serves, he told us was a drawing of where Gemma and I live. Gemma often prints out her own favourites, has them framed and hangs them on the walls of our home.

When the child next door starts crying, I stick on the Johnny Cash CD and twice read Little Patrick the story of *Abdul, Susie and the Lollipop*. The story is quite boring, so we drink another Long Island Iced Tea and examine his tractor and trailer. I put on my *Corpse Bride* DVD but Little Patrick doesn't like the look of the bride, so I watch it on my own. I consider putting on his DVD about the shark, but I have seen enough water for one day. Instead, we write two poems. One is for his granny who worries all the time. One is for his father who has a sore leg.

'When you get back to the farm, give your father a message from me', I say to Little Patrick, as our time together draws to a close. 'Tell him, soon the big house and all the fields will belong to Uncle Ronan'.

Later, after Little Patrick has been safely returned to his grateful parents, Gemma is still looking at the computer screen, flicking through her photographs. For a moment, she pauses at the one of Little Patrick at the pier, his uncertain expression before the swan, his bandaged thumb sticking into the winter air.

'Before he left he asked me how Johnny Cash fell into the ring of fire', I say.

'I think he enjoyed playing with you', says Gemma.

Soon, she switches on the TV. Barack is due to make one of his inspirational speeches and Gemma does not want to miss that. During the speech, Gemma hangs on every word. Afterwards, there are questions. Barack smiles at everyone who asks a question and says, 'yes we can'. I wish he would tell the reporters what he really thinks. Go to hell the lot of you. Shove your questions where the sun doesn't shine. Stop going on about things that are unsolvable. During my litany the phone rings. It's my sister, Jennifer.

'Cian is dying to see his Uncle Ronan', she says. 'Can you and Gemma take him for a night?'

'Yes we can', I say. 'Send him in on the train'.

That night, Gemma shudders when she thinks about Little Patrick on the pier wall. 'Don't talk about that', I say. 'It gives me the shivers'.

Instead, we resume the creation of our make-believe baby. Gemma adds a nice speaking voice. I give him an inquiring mind. To make things interesting, we weave a mesh of conflicting emotions into his curious psyche. If he wants to sit up and watch a horror movie we say of course you can Marlon and make room for him between us on the sofa. And if he wants to pack a rucksack and go see the world we say that is OK too and bid him a teary bon voyage. And, later again, in the soundless hours, when we catch ourselves not sleeping, and we ask each other where on earth he could be this quiet night, it's then that it hits us: that though he never cries, he has our hearts broken.

The Storyteller and the Thief

Last night a man on the news said the entire country is bankrupt. All the money is gone, he said with a smile on his face. We don't have a bean. He sounded as though he knew exactly what he was talking about, but when asked to explain why the country is now poor he just threw his arms into the air. Ma copied him and walked out of the room. I thought he had a terrific smile.

Nobody is in the mood for smiles these days. Ma isn't, that's for sure. Da has moved in with The Tarantula. Cora has gone to New Zealand. The number of pay-up letters the postman arrives with is driving her mad. 'Life is no longer a crystal staircase', she says. Boy, can she be a good victim.

Until last month she had a job in the library. It was only a part-time job but it got her out of the house three days a week. Then all the money disappeared, nobody was able to find it, and part-time workers in the library were told to go home and stay there.

It's a pity. They all loved her in the library. Especially the children during story hour. Ma used to read the story.

She did accents and sang when she felt like it, and performed gestures and crazy arm movements. You should have heard the children squeal.

The day she came home from the library and cried, the man from the bank was on the news. A voice was asking him questions. How much will you make this year? What has happened? Who can help? The man from the bank said he made three million euros last year, but this year he will make two million. None of us saw it coming, was his answer to the second question. I waited for the next answer but it never came. 'I'm at the end of my tether', Ma said and took to her bed.

She owes money to the bank, the Credit Union, NTL, the ESB, City Bin, the garage repair man, Statoil, her sister Bronagh and me. She writes down the name of everyone she owes and how much she owes on one of those yellow Post-its and sticks it to the fridge. Every day the list gets longer. Opening the fridge the other morning she broke off the door and wasn't able to put it back on. The call-out fee was eighty euros. Something happened with the oven too – pizzas started coming out black. Either the thing was broken or Ma is a worse cook than I had previously thought. Whatever the reason the man who came to look at the oven left a bill for one hundred and thirty-five euros. Then we had a cold spell and one of the pipes burst. Four hundred euros. To cap it all, we can't even pile into the car and drive away from everything because the pump that transfers petrol from the tank to the engine is broken, and the garage is refusing all contact with Ma until she pays for the new fan belt that was put in at the start of summer. I bet Da is delighted he moved out.

Answering the phone is my job. 'Say I am not here', Ma says when it rings. 'Say I am gone to the moon for the weekend'. She tells me to say this because she doesn't think the caller will go that far to collect his money. She gets me to answer the front door too. Even if it's only

Chancer Fay trying to sell his *Jesus Loves You* CDs or little Tommy Hanlon from next door looking for someone to chase him. These days Ma always expects the worst.

I like answering the phone. And I love putting the word Moon into sentences. Ma often uses it in the stories she tells. Especially in her opening line. *One night Eudora Cahill woke up beneath the gaze of a yellow moon. That night there was no moon but the stars were out, every single last one of them.* A line like either of those is always enough to get her into a story. Who knows where it may lead? Since finishing up in the library she hasn't told any stories. Not even an opening line. That's another pity.

Because we are now poor I steal things. Among other things, this month I have stolen a bag of Twirls from Mel Donlon's newsagents, a six-pack of Lucozade from the back yard of McMorrow's pub, three lemon meringues from Fionnuala Quirke's bakery, and when he wasn't looking, a cooked chicken from Slevin the butcher. Earlier, I managed to lay my hands on a tub of blueberries to help sweeten our daily porridge and a bottle of *Impulse* to help Ma smell nice.

I don't feel bad when I steal. Da once told me he was always at it when he was a young lad. Stealing silver spoons from hotels. Eating meals in restaurants without paying for them. Lifting trees off the bridge at Christmas time. According to Ma, those in charge of the country have been at it for years without anyone batting so much as an eyelid. 'No one gives a hoot', she says. Chances are no one is going to notice little me.

As it happens I'm really good at it. I have an honest face and really fast hands. Also, I've made friends with a security guard called Costello and a copper called Lawless. Any time I slip past them they smile and try to pat me on the head. If Da was still around he would be really proud of me. I say as much in the note I write to him in my room.

Da, you can be proud. I am now a criminal. Then Ma comes in to say good night and I ask her to tell me a story.

'I'm too tired to tell a story', she says. 'Now go to sleep and dream that none of this is happening'.

Instead of sleeping, I think about what I can steal for Ma's birthday. She is going to be forty-four the day after tomorrow, and I'd like to get her something really nice. Something that isn't edible or doesn't have to be sprayed. A scarf and gloves perhaps. A dress. Or something shiny. Once, I heard her say she likes shiny things. The display in Masterson's window is really shiny. I could get her something from there. One time Da got her a gold ring. But it went missing.

Last year she didn't get a thing. We all forgot. Cora's excuse was that she needed to save for New Zealand. My excuse was that I was busy composing a thank you note to great aunt Lucy for all the Chocolate Emeralds she had passed my way during her turbulent life. Da's excuse was that he was hardly ever around. He can use that as the same excuse this year.

I think Ma was disappointed we forgot. 'Just one small thing', I heard her say to her sister Bronagh on the phone. 'Some little thing, just to let me know they are aware I exist'. To take vengeance on us she became dangerous in the kitchen.

In the morning the phone is ringing.

'She's not here', I say to the man from the phone rental company. 'She's gone to the moon for the weekend'.

'That's my boy', she says when I hang up.

'Tell me a story', I say next, thinking it might be a good time. 'That's what you do best'.

'I have a pain in my head, kid', she says. 'No more stories'.

On my way to town I have an idea. I decide to pretend I am blind and beg. So I walk downtown tapping the ground with a stick. I make a note for myself too, and when I arrive there, sit down at the entrance to the shopping mall. I place my baseball cap on the ground and the note in front of it. *I am trying to save my eyes. Give generously.* I'm convinced I will make a fortune. In next to no time I'll be a top earner, featured in the Rich List given out free with Sunday newspapers.

Trouble is a few others have similar ideas. One of the drunks from the back lane. Someone else with a cardboard box and a note that says *homeless and hungry*. I wished I'd thought of that. They know the best places too, and they know that my eyes no more need saving than the man from the bank needs the money Ma owes him. 'Feck off', the homeless lad says to me and I don't need telling twice.

From Fionnuala Quirke's bakery I take three almond croissants. A French baguette. And some flapjacks. From the juice bar I take a pair of passion fruit smoothies. From the all-night pharmacy, a multi-pack of badly needed toothpastes and soaps. From Tesco I come away with soups and noodles. Pine nuts and honey. And several tubes of effervescent vitamin C which are really expensive and great for changing the flavour of the water.

On my way through the streets I think of more contenders for Ma's present. A candle and clock. A book of tasty recipes. A crate of Tylenol for the pain in her head. But I have a feeling Lawless is starting to see through my innocent smile. And everywhere I go Costello is hovering and waiting to pounce. 'Get the hell out of here, pipsqueak', Masterson growls at me when I step inside the jewellers. The birthday present will have to wait.

When I get home Ma is putting down the fire. She has briquettes, lumps of wood, a Zip lighter and a heap of paper sticks made from all the pay-up letters. 'Up the chimney is the place for them', she says. Then she tells me she's going hire a contract killer to take care of everyone she owes money to.

'You owe me money', I remind her.

'Well then you better watch out', she says and flicks a lit match.

When the fire gets going I stare into it. I listen to the bits of wood crackling, heap on more briquettes, watch smoke spiral up the chimney. I hold out my hands to the flames. They are yellow and orange and wave like flags in wind. They sound like flags too. When Ma goes into the kitchen I flick the tips of my fingers through the flames. But I don't feel anything. Not even a pinch.

Once the briquettes are gone I go in search of things to keep the fire going. My search takes me outside, into the garden, as far as the dead trees that run along the back lane. Chancer Fay is shaking his fist at one of them. He's trying to convince anyone who passes that ten-euro notes used to flutter on its leafless branches. I gather twigs, fallen branches, hunks of wood. I drag it all back to the house. I throw it all on the fire.

'What are you doing, you crazy boy?' Ma howls at me.

'I'm keeping you warm', I say and she laughs.

That night I try for a story.

'Make it up', I plead. 'It doesn't have to be a long one. Something short will do. For old times' sake'.

'Forget it', she says. 'My storytelling days are behind me'.

She walks out of the room and pulls the door closed behind her. I try to think of one of the stories from her days in the library, one that will help me go to sleep. But her sobbing in the next room distracts me. Instead, I think of Da's theory. He once told it to me when he was drinking gin. Everybody in our family was born with a flaw, he said. Some little thing working against them. We may not even know we have this flaw. We could go through our entire life and not know what it is, Da said.

'What's your flaw?' I asked him.

'How the hell should I know?' he said, and took a mouthful of gin.

'What's Cora's flaw?' I asked him.

'How the hell should I know?' he said, and took another mouthful of gin.

'What's Ma's flaw?' I asked him.

'Don't get me started', he said, and refilled his glass. I miss him.

'She's not here', I say when the man from the bank calls up. 'She's gone to the moon for the weekend'.

'It's not the weekend, it's Tuesday morning', the bank man says.

'Well I'll be sure to pass that on to her when she gets back', I say and hang up.

'What would I do without you?' she says.

'You owe me twelve euros', I remind her.

'Watch what you say, young man. I will have you shot first thing'. Too late, I have already hit the streets.

I take a trip through the shopping mall. I'm sure I will find a dress there. I try *Modern Mum, Happening Woman* and *Elegant Undies*. A starving stick insect wouldn't fit inside the things on display. Next, I take a look inside *Healing Earth.* In there they have colourful Worry Boxes, huge Make-a-Wish dice, and a selection of fridge magnets that say things like *when the going gets tough the tough eat chocolate.* Then I stroll into *Beauty by Helen.* All she has are vouchers for face mapping, eyebrow shaping, back exfoliation, skin brightening, an all-over massage and something called a Brazilian that guarantees to leave only a landing strip – whatever that means.

Masterson is resting his head on his crossed arms when I tiptoe inside his shop. I head straight for the shiny thing I'd spotted before. I slip it out of its velvet cushion and let it slide deep inside my pocket. Happy Birthday Ma, I whisper, turning for the door, I've even turned the handle when I feel the strong arm on my shoulder.

'Does your mother ever answer the phone?' Lawless asks me when he pokes his head into the room he's left me inside. I look up at him and shake my head No.

'Is there anything you want?' he asks next. Without looking up I ask for a pen and paper. 'Ah, so you want to write a confession', he says with a chuckle before returning with a pad.

Dear Da, I begin when I'm left by myself again, but my mind wanders to another theory Da told me. He used to read the Old Testament. He knew stories from it. His favourite was the one about Lot and his wife fleeing the doomed city of Sodom. As they flee they are warned not to look back. So Lot's wife looks back and turns into a pillar of salt. 'That story says it all', Da said. 'Always remember: when you run, don't look back. If you are woman you will turn into a pillar of salt. If you are a man you will only see pillars of salt'.

'Ma is the storyteller', I told him, when he'd finished.

'Be like that so', he said, then poured himself a gin.

Eventually Ma shows up at the station. I can hear her voice as she is led through. In the room I'm in there's a fly bumping on and off the bare yellow bulb. A reek of stale cigarettes drifts through the air. A taste of rank cheese. Ma sits into the chair across from me. She stares at the floor. Then she notices the pen and paper on the table between us, and she leans in for a closer look at what I've written. When she's finished reading she pushes the note back over my side of the table, sits back into her chair and draws a deep breath. 'For many nights there was nothing to do except gaze at the moon', she begins. Already I can tell it's going to be a great story.

PSYCHOTIC EPISODES

'What day is it today, then?' Fleming asks me as he pops his Olanzapine. 'I keep thinking it's a Tuesday'.

'I'm going with Wednesday', I say, and gurgle down my Duloxetine.

We like discussing the calendar when we take medication.

They tell us we are lucky to be here. The people here can work miracles, they say. The food isn't bad either. And the views. From our rooms there are views to die for. Not that I've noticed.

Olanzapine is supposed to stave off anxiety. Who are they trying to kid? It barely delays the voices. But there's no talking to them. Instead, it increases my appetite. I have ballooned so much I bob. Watch out, one or two call out when I head towards them. Others grunt and flick me away. Duloxetine is supposed to cheer us up. Fleming laughs at that and asks do they stock Hitler's gas. Then he falls asleep. Fleming falls asleep everywhere.

Sometimes we swap days. Fleming takes Wednesday, and I take Tuesday. Sometimes we swap medication. When we do we become fat and tired together, then duck out to the garden, lie down side by side among the rose bushes and nap. Oh look, they say when they find us, the heavy sleepers.

But most of the time we just drift. Around here we like to travel incognito.

To pass time Fleming and I have decided to make a TV show. Television is the place to be, says Fleming.

As it's just the two of us we're having to multi-task. I'm going to be producer and clapper loader. Fleming's taking care of direction and dolly grip. We will co-edit, script together and be executives in charge of everything else, especially catering. As yet, we haven't decided on a title for the show. Nor do we have a concept. According to Fleming this doesn't matter. All we need is one episode. The pilot, Fleming calls it. When we pitch, Fleming is sure they will jump all over our pilot. After that, it's all gravy.

'I think we should pitch on Thursday', says Fleming.

'It can't be Thursday', I remind him. 'It has to be Tuesday or Wednesday'.

'What's it like in Lula land?' he says next.

Fleming loves asking me that. Sometimes I wake up and gasp *my parents christened me Lula*. Even then, they must have known. Early on, Fleming confessed the only reason he talks to me is because he likes my name. He loves my name. This is good. He doesn't talk to anyone else. He throws punches. He does this because he is unpredictable. When he dies, he says he wants *they forced me underground* put on his headstone.

He has an interest in American presidents. His interest has worked its way into the TV show we want to make.

Suddenly he has come up with a concept. He now also has a title: *Once elected all they do is watch television*. For example, when Iraq and Iran go to war Ronald Reagan is watching *Little House on the Prairie* in the Oval Office. Next door, in the War Room, the generals are worried about a battle going off without them. They are bristling. But Ronald isn't budging. I'm not getting involved until *Little House on the Prairie* is over, Fleming has Ronald say in the script. And Nancy, tell those boys in the War Room to keep it down.

In another episode, just as trouble is kicking off in Somalia, Bill Clinton is watching *The Simpsons*. Homer, Homer, Homer, Fleming has Bill say with a finger wag and subsequent chuckle. Then, just before hell breaks loose in Afghanistan, George W Bush is watching *The Sopranos* – with his father. Hey pops, have you any idea what's happening? Fleming has George W ask his father who is sound asleep.

'I think we should shorten the title to *Once Elected*', I suggest when Fleming asks what I think.

'Lula, I could kiss you', Fleming says, beaming. Then we go and eat.

I feel full after every meal. Minutes after my last mouthful, I tiptoe to the bathroom, tie back my hair, remove my finger rings, lift the toilet seat, lean over and shove my hand down my throat.

It's all in my head, they try telling me, but I know *that's* not true.

Later, the sugar cravings send me to the vending machine in the foyer. When I arrived here I had a biscuit tin containing three hundred and fifty-five euros in change. It's dwindling fast.

'Try garlic', says Fleming when he sees me scoffing. 'Four cloves every day and you'll never look at a Mars bar in the same way again'.

Once, I remember seeing my father throw a cup of tea in my mother's face. What I can't recall is what happened next. At some point I did have a thought: Eating is too risky.

Fleming knows things. As soon as he has finished scripting the Bill Clinton episode he says: 'You know the little Simpson kid – Maggie her name is – the one who is always sucking the soother. In one episode she speaks a word and guess who they have do the voice? Go on guess. Guess three times'. I guess twice and give up. 'Elizabeth Taylor', he says with satisfaction.

'Who's Elizabeth Taylor, Fleming?' I ask.

'Elizabeth Taylor is my favourite psychotic', he says.

'Where do I come?'

'Fourth', he says.

Fleming tells me each 'president' in *Once Elected* is based on someone from his own family. Ronald is his kind-hearted but forgetful grandfather. Bill is his incredibly bright but can't keep-it-in-his-pants father. And George W is his daughter.

'You have a daughter?' I say to Fleming.

'Oh yes', he says. 'I wish she was more reflective'.

'Which one is Fleming?' I ask.

'I'm thinking Obama', he replies.

'The visionary'.

'Got it in one, kid'.

'And what TV show is he watching?'

'We'll have to wait until Korea launches the missile', Fleming says, but this time I think he's trying to dodge the question.

Family talk is not my strong point. I erased them from my memory during a moment of clarity when I was seventeen, working in a bank and contemplating a massacre.

'I was once in a bank', Fleming says. 'I think I was seven. Stick 'em up, I said. Everyone laughed'.

Fleming tells me he passed out twice out when he was little. Once for two minutes. Once for four. The four-minute stretch was enough to have them declare him clinically dead. His brain was starved for four minutes. This is one reason for his vulnerability, he says. Why he is easily led.

A doctor once listened to my story and concluded I didn't like myself very much. The following week the same doctor was found in his bedroom, dangling from a rope. *The world is a hospital* someone told me he had put down in his goodbye note – among other things.

As an aid to all the medication and talk-talk therapy, they show us reruns of Laurel and Hardy flicks. Fleming says: when Stan Laurel was on his death bed he was surrounded by some glum individuals. Say, said Stan, if any of you lot cry at my funeral I'll never speak to you again.

'He was one to talk', I say.

The other day I took a stab at making an ornamental mirror. To encourage my efforts I was provided with a supply of glitter-stones, heavy-duty glue and five-by-seven cuts of hardboard. It lasted until I ran out of glitter stones. 'Get your self some more', they told me, but I had already seen enough.

A lot of the time I think awful things, but not necessarily about myself. I think: wouldn't it be great to push somebody from a high window. Hammer a nail into a forehead. Tie down a powerful man, and use him as a trampoline. I don't want to think these things, but can't help myself. Yesterday, a guy with a funny mouth and a voice I jumped back from told me to stop being narcissistic. 'Narcissistic?' I repeated after him and was encouraged to ransack my bad mind for clues as to what this could possibly mean. Nuts to that idea. Instead, I glared at Funny Mouth and said, *this is what it's like in Lula land, fucker.*

Sometimes I think: A demon is in charge of me.

'Crazy minds think alike', Fleming says when we are lying out among the rose bushes. 'And shrinks seldom differ'.

'Are you crazy?' I ask him, and he nods. I prefer making trips to the weighing scales and the bathroom mirror.

When I mention the pains in my head they start talking about finding something to send my intrusive thoughts packing. I think they think that if they stumble upon the correct medication the cause won't matter. Stumble. That's an interesting word to use. I must ask Fleming what he knows about it. After what I said to the shrink I am now his third favourite.

In the afternoon we attend group therapy. 'Look at that mountain over there', Fleming says, staring through the window of our meeting room. 'Some day I might climb that mountain'.

During group therapy we have to make a resolution or outline an ambition. Fleming says: I would like to win an Emmy. I say: I am going to execute every last motherfucking one of you. In the resulting mayhem I let rip with my ornamental mirror and Fleming throws a punch. 'You are now my second favourite', Fleming whispers to me as the goons pin us down.

They are worried about my mouth. What's coming out every time I open it. Also, they have found sweet wrappers under a broken floorboard in my room. Empty bags of Chipsticks. I told them I want to want to get better. It's a start, they conceded.

'Now what would you like to eat?' they ask us when we pop our pills.

'I'll have six sandwiches with something different in each of them', says Fleming.

'I'll have one sandwich with Divilly's turkey and Branston Pickle', I say.

We're like chalk and cheese, really.

'Fleming', I say, during our meal. 'Do you think I'm narcissistic?'

'Now that's a question for the mirror you're always looking at', he says.

'Fleming', I say. 'Is Elizabeth Taylor really psychotic?'

'She won an Oscar for it', he replies.

Fleming also says he's had enough. He can't take any more.

'Tonight, I'm checking out of this hotel, kid', he tells me. 'This is no place for an agitated mind. I belong on HBO'.

'What are you going to do?' I ask him. 'Throw the fridge through a window'.

'Watch it, kid', he says. 'Around here, I make the jokes'.

'Who's joking?' I say. And then: 'Can I come?'

'What star sign are you?' he asks me.

'Sagittarius', I reply.

'Forget it', he says. 'Sagittarians are unwieldy'.

I'm so mad I go straight to the goons. By now, they don't want to believe a Holy Mary coming out of my mouth. All the same they catch him red-handed, praise my vigilance, and decide that perhaps it's better if we are kept apart.

Before he is carted out of here, he asks for me. 'It looks like Korea is ready to fire the rocket', he says.

'So, tell me', I say. 'Which show is Obama watching?'

He smiles at me at then, it takes years off him. 'Ask me a tricky one some time, kid'. Then he winks and whispers the name of our show.

That night I make another ornamental mirror. When I'm done I place it on the window sill, and get ready to take a good look at myself. But it's the mountain beyond that catches my eye, lit up beneath the gaze of a yellow moon. 'Anybody wanting to climb that must be crazy', I tell the moon. And with either hand I grip the window sill to stop myself from shaking.

WOMEN DRIVERS ON TAYLOR'S HILL

The first time it happened I was on my way to the hospital to see my father. He was weak and frail and didn't have long to live. My brother in London had no interest in coming over. My brother in New York was too busy making money. My third and final brother was wandering through hills in Nepal, and didn't want to be contacted. They were an interesting, if self-centred bunch, my brothers, and it saddened me that they had come to have such little regard. I was mulling all this over on my bicycle, freewheeling down Taylor's Hill, when I slammed into the car door.

It was my own fault really. I should have known better than to set off down the hill on a school day afternoon. Especially at half past two. It was when school finished for the day and, in order to pick up their little boys and girls from the school at the bottom of the hill, parents tended to park wherever they could along this stretch of the narrowing road. It was a tricky stretch at the quietest of times. The crossroads junction usually generated a lot of fist-waving, the lights were erratic, something unforeseeable was always likely to happen. Even so, I should have known that this woman was going to open out her car door as I sped by.

You could be doing worse for yourself, Enda, I told myself a few moments after I had landed on my arm, and was wiggling back into place the small fragment of bone that had come away from the tip of my elbow.

'I'm OK, lady', I said, as she looked down at me from where she was standing.

'You were going very fast', she said.

'Don't I know it', I said, rubbing some blood out of my nose and glancing over at my flattened bicycle. 'Every time I come down that hill I seem to pick up speed'.

'Well, be more careful next time', she said and hurried off in the direction of the school.

My dad had a tumour in his kidney. Last time they checked it was roughly the size of a tennis ball. They told me if they took it out there wouldn't be much of him left. He was now enjoying the morphine. I had asked my London brother to come over when I explained the situation. Mark, I said, he will be gone in six weeks. It might be good for you two to speak before the end. But he had no interest. There had been a lot of stuff between them back in the day, stuff Mark wasn't ready to let go. All I could do was keep him informed.

Paul, my New York brother, was rich and said he might be able to fly over closer to the end. It all depended on how things went with a project he was currently busy with. Until he had some key people on board his hands were tied. This was the kind of language Paul spoke, had been speaking for a long time, and I found it difficult to convey what it was I wanted to say to him.

Anthony, my wandering brother, remained out of contact. He was the youngest of the four of us and since our mother's death several years ago was searching for a meaning to his life. His search had taken him to many faraway places, places I doubted I'd ever get to see. But so far none of them had turned up this special meaning he was looking for.

I was going over all of this in my head during my next cycling trip in to the hospital, coasting the wraparound swerves, doing my best to flee the cut-stone walls that always tried to close me in. By the time I was coming down the hill I was trying to figure out a way to entice my London brother over to see our dad one last time and I was hoping that things worked out smoothly with my New York brother's business project and I was wondering how hard it might be to get a message through to Anthony when I was clobbered by a woman in a jeep who claimed she was trying to overtake me.

For a minute I had no idea what was happening. On the ground beside me I could see my bicycle, the ticking spokes of the back wheel, the warped front tyre, a broken pedal. Luckily, I had landed on my kneecap – already I could feel blood seeping out of it – but at least I had spared my brittle elbow. From her driver's seat, the woman in the jeep was calling out something to me.

'You didn't leave me much room', she said, leaning slightly towards me.

'You're probably right', I said, rolling up my trouser leg for a look at the damage. 'I have an unhappy knack for veering out at the wrong moment'.

'I'm in a rush', she said, glancing down at my leg. 'I have to be somewhere else'.

'It's only a scratch', I said, dabbing at the blood with the handkerchief I had fetched out of my trousers pocket. 'Off you go now. No harm done. But be careful, lady. Watch out for crazy cyclists'.

She revved unusually loudly, sped away and drove for a further fifty yards or so, then swung her cumbersome vehicle expertly up onto the footpath alongside the school railings, just beating a driver approaching from the other direction to the last remaining parking gap. I picked myself up off the ground, gathered my damaged bicycle and made my way to the repair shop.

You should get yourself a car, my New York brother had said to me several times over the course of the past year. Hell, I'll even spot you the price of one, Paul said. That's really generous of you, Paul, I said, but I don't need a car. Really, I don't, I continued when I heard the sighing coming through the receiver. And it was true. I didn't need a car. Didn't want a car. I was grateful to him for the gesture. Save your money, I told him.

'Oh my God! You poor thing', the repair man said when I introduced him to my damaged bicycle.

'It could have been worse', I said.

'Worse!' he said, bringing his hands to his face. 'What happened? No, wait. Don't tell me. I've had a rough day'. He had taken the bicycle from me and was cradling the handlebars. He knelt down to take a closer look at the mangled tyre. He gently placed his greasy hand on the chain. At any moment he is going to burst into tears I thought.

'How soon do you need it?' the repair man asked me as soon as he managed to compose himself.

'Could you have it by tomorrow?' I asked him. 'I'd like to get in to town to get some things'.

'I will try', he said. 'But I must warn you – I am not a miracle worker. There are many bicycles needing repairs – as you can see'.

The repair man took my bicycle and carefully carried it into his work area where it took its place amongst a large assortment of bicycles in various states of disrepair. Punctures. Broken chains. Loose brakes. Gear problems.

Damaged handlebars. Wrecked frames. It was all there, right in front of me. The repair man knew it too, and he shook his head sadly as he made a forlorn patrol of his workshop.

Later, I called Mark and told him dad was fading fast. He's not going to be conscious for much longer I said. Is there anything you want me to say, Mark? I asked my brother. A message I can pass on. There was a momentary silence at the other end, and I thought he was trying to form some parting words. Something that might go a little way towards mending the rift that had come between them all that time ago. It still wasn't too late and that's how I thought Mark was starting to see things. No, he finally said into the silence. There is nothing. Then he hung up. Things weren't going so smoothly in New York either. People are dragging their heels Paul told me when I called him. Negotiating this deal is going to take some finessing. Call me again in an hour or two, he said. I might have some more news then. After that I wondered if I should get in touch with Anthony. I paced the kitchen, tried to locate the seven or eight numbers Anthony had passed my way over the past few years. I rang two or three of them but the number was either no longer in service or made sinister noises at the other end and so I gave up. Later again, when I put in another call to New York, I was informed everything was moving quickly towards the edge of a very high cliff.

'This is a strong bicycle', the repair man said when I appeared the following day. He was proudly wheeling my bicycle towards me and nodding approvingly at it. 'I would love a bicycle like this. They don't make them like they used to, you know. They don't make them to last. This will last', he said, gripping the handlebars firmly and jerking them in my direction.

'I hope it lasts', I said. 'We get along very well together'.

'I want you to make me a promise', he said, clutching onto the handlebars.

'Yes?'

'Promise me you'll look after her. Promise me you won't let anything bad happen'. He had a look of intense pleading in his eyes and he was very reluctant to let go the handlebars.

'I'll try', I said, doing my best to reclaim my bicycle. 'But you know how it is – it's a jungle out there'.

My dad went steadily downhill. He became very reliant on the morphine and the nurse showed him how to administer it in order that he may avail of relief as and when he needed it. He was very liberal with dosages and gradually he lapsed into a coma, whereupon the nurse and I resumed morphine duty. Throughout it all I kept my London brother informed and listened to my New York brother's mounting exasperation as business negotiations deteriorated and then completely broke down. Anthony remained out of reach.

Things also went steadily worse for me and my bicycle. Another woman tried to overtake me, and in her eagerness to do so, she forgot to move out and her Mercedes rear-ended my bicycle, sending me over the handlebars and then crashing down on the crown of my head. 'I know, I know', I said to her, trying not to let my momentary double vision interfere with my train of thought. 'I should be wearing a helmet. If I had been the loud ringing inside me wouldn't be as bad. Off you go now, I'm sure you have important things to do'.

Another day, the woman overtaking me did move out, but as soon as she overtook me a parking gap became available and in her eagerness to secure it she cut me off and once again I was sailing through air.

Moments later I was on the ground, in the middle of the road. Traffic had declared a temporary ceasefire. There wasn't a moving vehicle in sight. All I could see was the lush bloom of youthful trees, gates of walled-off gardens, the bay windows of the period houses I had always envied along this stretch of road. To my astonishment I was in one piece, and, my gushing lip aside, didn't feel much pain. I looked around and cast a sympathetic gaze at my bicycle. Then, something that didn't occur every day happened. My mobile phone went off and when I pressed the answer button to my amazement I heard Anthony, my wandering brother, on the other end. The line was a little fuzzy, but there was no mistaking my younger brother's voice.

'Anthony! Jesus, how the hell are you?' I said, finding it difficult to contain my excitement. 'How goes it with the Nepal Hills?'

'I'm good, bro', he said. 'The hills are great. Listen, can you talk?'

'Talk? Of course I can talk', I said, spitting away some gouts of blood.

'Listen, bro, I wanted you to be the first to know. I think I've found it. I think this is the place'.

'You've found it! Jesus, that's great, Anthony'.

'Yes, it is. Listen to me, bro. I'm not coming home. Now that I've found it I have to stay here. Are you listening to me? And I've met someone. Someone special'.

'Someone special! That's brilliant, Anthony'.

'Can you tell the old man? Can you tell him I won't be coming home?'

'Well, I'll try, Anthony, but he isn't good. It's unlikely he'll pull through'.

'I'll write him a letter. And I'll send a photograph. Tell him that, won't you'.

'I will, brother', I said, 'but, listen to me, now. I have to tell you something'.

Then the line started to break up. I couldn't make out what else he was saying and when I tried to let him know about what was happening at this end the static became too much. He was gone before I had a chance to mention our dad.

When I made it into the hospital my dad's nurse was good enough to stitch my lip back together again. 'I think you need to find a different route', she said to me as she tenderly wove her magic.

The last time it happened was the day my father died. This time the woman overtaking me moved out and stayed out, but whether it was something being said to her through the mobile phone she had clamped to her ear, or something to do with the shaking fist of the old man on the footpath she had mounted during the overtaking manoeuvre, she didn't notice that an oncoming car had had to swerve in order to avoid a collision. And so quickly did this second car swerve and so lost was I in thoughts of morphine dosages and Nepal hills and the cut and thrust of New York business deals, that I didn't swing out of the way in time. And everything went black.

Eventually I regained consciousness. I had landed twenty feet or so from where my bicycle now lay, its back wheel ticking over, the front a mangled mess, and was picturing the sorry look the repair man would have on his face upon my imminent appearance at his shop when the woman started shouting.

'Oh my God!' I could hear her say. She was kneeling over me, a rich blend of perfume, make-up and moisturiser. She had streaky blonde hair and startling blue eyes. For a moment I wondered if I was still unconscious and was dreaming. Then my head started to pound.

'Can you move?' she said to me. She was staring intensely down at me.

'You're beautiful', I said, looking back up.

'You've had a bang on the head. I saw it. It can't be good. We need to get you to the hospital'.

'That's right', I said. 'That's where I was headed'.

'What?'

'My dad. He has only days left. Hours even. I'm on my way to say goodbye'.

'Oh my God! I'm so sorry', the woman said. She looked very worried. It made her more beautiful to me.

'Don't be sorry', I said. 'It's not your fault'.

'I'm so sorry I hit you. I'm so sorry I knocked you down. I'm taking you to the hospital right now'.

'I think you're beautiful', I said again, suddenly grateful for my returning double vision. 'I think you are the most beautiful thing I have ever seen'.

'You've had a bang on the head. It could be serious. Let's get you to the hospital'.

'Oh! What's the rush?' I said. 'Let me sit here awhile and look at you'.

With her help, I managed to manoeuvre myself into a sitting position. Then she was on her mobile phone, talking to someone, but I could only vaguely hear what she was saying. Everything around me was going in slow motion. Little colourless circles floated in front of my eyes. I reached out a finger and tried to pop one.

'We'll have you at the hospital in no time', I heard her say again.

'Are you married?' I asked her. 'The last two to knock me down, I'm fairly sure they were married. One of them didn't stick around, so I didn't get a chance to ask her. It doesn't matter. I don't think I want to marry her. Are you married?'

'I'm engaged to be married'.

'Oh, please don't say that. You are so beautiful. I want you to know that'.

'And you need help. And it's on the way. So hang in there, OK'.

'All I'm saying is that sometimes a man can sit back and admire. He can sit back and say, now that is a beautiful thing. Who are you getting married to? I bet he's a shining light in his chosen field. I once wanted to be a journalist. A feature writer. Did I tell you, you are the third woman to knock me down this week? I didn't get a good look at the other two. I'm sure they are beautiful in their own way. But you are in a league of your own. I'm giving you the prize. Hey, that's a nice car you have there. What make of car is that?'

'What?'

'Your car. What is it?'

'It's – eh – an Audi'.

'An Audi. My dad used to have an Audi. He was emotional about it. Are you really going through with it?'

'Through with what?'

'The wedding. I don't think you should. I think you should have second thoughts'.

'You've had a knock on your head. Please try to relax. We'll have you at the hospital very soon. I promise we will. Everything will be OK. You'll see'.

I was hearing these comforting words, but I had no idea where they were coming from. I was sitting in the middle of the road with a beautiful woman and my head was thumping and I was counting the floating circles and other cars were negotiating a way around us and I was hearing more comforting words and I knew then my father was dead and all I wanted was to look into the woman's eyes.

And suddenly she was crying. Large tears, dignified and unstoppable, sprung from her eyes and dropped down off her face and landed on the ground between us.

'I'm a horrible person', she said through her sobbing. 'I'm a horrible person and now I've knocked you down'.

'That's not true', I said, but she wasn't listening to me. Her tears, still coming, were large and fell like pieces of clear snow. Her eyes glistened, she wrapped her arms around herself and it made her more beautiful to me again. 'I'm a useless person', she said.

'Come here to me', I said, overwhelmed now, by an immense pity for this stranger unlucky enough to have crossed my path. 'Come here', I said, reaching out my arms to her and drawing her towards me. She went limp in my arms and I rocked her gently and I could feel her sobbing and all the time I was feeling more and more lightheaded.

'You're not useless', I said, wrapping my arms further around her. 'You're a beautiful person. You're beautiful, and you're saving my life'.

BLEEDING BOY

The summer my mother died Heff became my best friend. His name was Heffernan, that's why he was called Heff. Heff could tell you what song was number one the week you were born and do the Rubik's cube in fifty-three seconds. He had a pool table in his bedroom. He was tall and great at telling jokes. For much of that summer the last things I was in the mood for were jokes but when Heff told one I laughed. He played basketball too. That's where we first met – at the courts.

A few weeks after becoming best friends we made a list each of our favourite women. After wading through photographs of pop singers and supermodels in magazines, after countless close studies of girls who bounced around our neighbourhood, we confined our selections to mothers living along our road. This was Heff's idea. This was a list that hadn't been made before, he said. In our friendship, as well as being the joke teller, he was the ideas man.

Very quickly we both had a top five. We differed on numbers two, three and four, but we agreed on number one.

Mrs Cassidy.

Mrs Cassidy was gorgeous. She was young for a mother, had brown hair that curved into her neck, her lips were moist and plump. She wore singlets with glittery writing and short denim skirts. She had a tattoo on her right shoulder. Her husband was a car salesman and looked like a toad. 'What is she doing with him?' Heff demanded to know. The way he asked it I thought he wouldn't sleep until he was given an answer that satisfied him. It was a question that had no answer and my friend agonised restlessly.

Shortly after I began calling for Heff, Mrs Cassidy smiled at me when we passed each other in the street. It was a lovely smile, friendly and kind, and her lips pouted just before the smile, as though she was considering whether or not I deserved one. I wanted to stop and have a conversation with her. Get to know her a little better. See what sort of a personality she had. But I knew I would be tongue-tied.

I said nothing to Heff about my encounter. I wanted to keep the vision of that smile all for myself, and assemble an entire personality around it. Usually, if you said a girl had a good personality that was code for saying she looked like the back of a tractor. That was Heff's phrase. He had one for every occasion. But after receiving that smile from Mrs Cassidy I knew the codebook could be torn up. Her smile, and the obvious things about her, made her the perfect woman. That was another thing Heff had going that summer. According to Heff, to be perfect a woman had to have three things. A good face. A good body. And a good personality. 'He drives a hard bargain', my father said when I told him Heff's terms. 'You haven't seen Mrs

Cassidy recently', I whispered, which was true – that summer he had barely set foot outside the door of our house.

At night I lay awake and thought of Heff and his lists and Mrs Cassidy and her smile. Then I thought of my mother. She had always been making lists. She'd had a useless memory, so she used to buy yellow notepads that had a sticky strip on one side. On these notes she would write her lists and then stick them to the fridge door or the kitchen wall, wherever there was space. She wrote lists of little things she had to do. Pay the ESB. Order oil. Pick up a Walsh's loaf, which my father and I quickly devoured. One time she forgot to bring home the Walsh's loaf. She had stopped off at a telephone box to make a call and she had left the loaf behind her. At the time, a notorious member of the IRA was being held in the town barracks before being sent up north. *Release him or there'll be trouble* a message had been phoned in. And when my mother remembered where she had left her Walsh's loaf and returned to pick it up, the phone box was surrounded by soldiers with guns. Meantime, two members of the bomb squad were kneeling just outside the box and were prodding the Walsh's loaf with long metal wands. We often laughed about that.

Her big list was a list of places she wanted to see before she died. The Grand Canyon. The Great Wall of China. Berlin. She wrote it all down, said she was going to cross off each item one by one after she got to see it. I kept her list. I had it in my top drawer. I thought that maybe some day I'd get to one or two of these places. Then I could cross them off.

Mrs Cassidy's first name was Maria. She lived next door to Heff. If it was sunny she stripped into a yellow bikini and sunbathed in a full-length deck chair in her back garden. Sometimes she wore a white bikini. I liked the white bikini.

Heff liked the yellow. We disagreed on some things and bikini colour was one of them. Because we were best friends our disagreement didn't come between us. 'Let's go and look at our favourite woman', Heff would say if a little tension crept in to our discussions. He always knew how to resolve things.

Maria Cassidy had brown skin. It was smooth and lovely and watching her from Heff's bedroom window was both great fun and painful. I ached when I looked down at Maria Cassidy. She was the most beautiful thing. She wore sunglasses, and made herself a fizzy drink with a straw and set it down on the grass beside her. From time to time, she reached an arm over, grabbed her drink, brought it to her plump lips and sipped through the straw. She rubbed suntan lotion all over her arms and legs. Her legs went on forever. The sunglasses made her mysterious.

'I'm going to throw myself into that chair and rub my face all over it', Heff said as soon as Maria Cassidy got up and went inside. I hadn't reached that far. I was still with her smile. It had stayed with me after passing her on the street. And I continued to think of it as I passed her house on my way home at night.

It was quiet in our house that summer. My father sat up late. He watched news reports, sometimes a late film. Often he sat by the open fireplace holding his head in his hands. I found it harder and harder to talk to him. It was always late when I came home from Heff's house and I hoped my father would be in bed by the time I got in. But he was almost always still up.

As I lay in bed I said her name into the darkness. Maria Cassidy. I thought her name was very exotic. I pictured her on a yacht somewhere, lying out on deck in her white bikini, clear blue waters shimmering, that lucky sun gazing down on her all day. Making her smile.

After a while I tried to think of my mother's smile. It wasn't as vivid as Maria Cassidy's and the pain that came was different to the pain I felt when I thought of Maria Cassidy. As more summer nights passed, thoughts of my mother and the pain that came with those thoughts began to fade. At first I thought this was a good thing. Then her smile began to fade and I wasn't so sure.

When Maria Cassidy took some time off from sunbathing, Heff and I watched Kevin Ford's driving tricks. He drove a Honda and it had a souped-up engine, go-fast stripes and spoilers. We sat down on the curb and watched his performance. Little Stephen Cassidy and his sister Ciara sat down beside us and watched too. They were always together, running up and down our road, chasing Mrs Redihan's dog, sometimes crossing the road one after the other, and making for the muck hole at the top of the grassy bank. Ciara was always first across the road, and Stephen always followed her. 'He looks just like his mother. He's going to have a great time when he's older', Heff said about Stephen.

Behind the steering wheel of his Honda, Kevin Ford was soon busy. He revved and spun around and skidded and reversed and did another handbrake spin around. Eventually, Maria Cassidy or one of the other mothers came out on to the road and told Kevin Ford to take his loud car somewhere else. This made Kevin mad, you could see him grimacing behind his steering wheel, his grip on it tightening, and he revved his engine until it reached the point of no return and he sped away, the Honda's exhaust coughing out a black cloud of smoke which spread a suffocating stench through the air. After watching Maria Cassidy in her back garden the entire show was a real let down.

Luckily, the sun continued to shine. Every day was hotter than the one before.

'I am going to melt if this weather continues', said Mrs Redihan who lived next door to my father and me, and she tugged at the cardigan she was wearing.

'Let her melt', Heff said. 'The world can continue without the removal of that cardigan'.

Other mothers along our road made the most of the rising temperatures. One or two of them put on bathing suits. Some paraded about in bikinis. Heff said he'd run away from home if his mother pulled a stunt like that. Either that or he was going to find a gun and shoot himself. Between throwing himself out of bedroom windows and now all this gun-talk he was becoming very fatalistic. I didn't think his mother was *that* bad.

There were so many different shapes. Heff and I responded to most of them. They all looked wonderful in that everything-is-new way, and with each passing day Heff and I happily noted the appearance of a new bikini along our road. Deep down, however, we both knew that none of them would ever be able to compete with Maria Cassidy. During that hot summer of mothers in bikinis, suntan lotion and neverending legs she kept one step ahead.

When she lay on her stomach, reached her arms around and untied the straps of her bikini top – the yellow one – Heff had to leave his bedroom window and go into the bathroom. I stayed at the window, staring down at her, and concentrated on her shoulders. They looked delicate and strong. The ends of her hair touched them. I wanted to touch them too. I said as much to Heff when he emerged, red-faced, from the bathroom. For a few minutes he stared intensely down at her. Unusually for him he didn't say a word, and I thought to myself, *this is it, out the window he goes*. But he didn't jump. Instead, he became hot and bothered once again, and made another trip to the bathroom.

'To think that slimy toad gets to crawl all over her', Heff said when we sat out on the curb to cool off and saw Mr Cassidy come home from a day selling cars. We didn't really cool off, though, we never did. But, after one of our sessions with Maria Cassidy, we needed some time out of doors.

'Is Grimshaw still your number two?' I asked him.

'Yeah. Her face isn't great, but she has a good body'.

'Brady is my number two'.

'She has a good personality. Her face is pleasant, but I'm not sure about the rest. Have a look at Grimshaw. She's in a bikini this week – well, half of her is'.

We stopped talking then. Kevin Ford's Honda growled past us, skidded and spun around, narrowly avoiding Mrs Redihan's dog. Mrs Redihan came out of her house and shook a fist at Kevin Ford's Honda. Behind his steering wheel Kevin rolled his eyes. Heff and I stood up, and headed back to Heff's bedroom until the sun went down.

After it got dark Heff and I played pool and a card game Heff had invented. From time to time, he put me on stopwatch duty while he scrambled his Rubik's cube and then tried to beat his record. As he potted balls he asked me to give him some dates so that he could make sure he knew what song had been number one.

'The 22nd of November 1960', I gave him.

'*It's Now or Never*, Elvis Presley', he answered without a pause for thought.

'The 7th of September 1970', I gave him.

'*Tears of a Clown*, Smokey Robinson and The Miracles', he said.

'The 10th of August 1977'.

'*I Feel Love*, Donna Summer'.

'June First 1983'.

'That's too recent. Give me a hard one. Wait, isn't that the date your mother –'

He didn't finish the sentence. Instead, he moved straight on to one of his jokes, one he had already told, one I had laughed loudly at. I laughed loudly again this time – so loudly that Heff's mother woke up and shooed me out of there.

When I was walking home from Heff's, I saw a squad car outside Kevin Ford's house. Lots of people were milling about in the front garden, drinking and smoking. A couple were groping each other in the back seat of Kevin's Honda. On his doorstep two guards were talking to Kevin who was waving his arms and shaking his head vigorously. Those in the garden were loud and the guards were telling them to clear off. I continued on my way home. I was in no mood for a party. Further on, I saw Mrs Redihan at her window, her curtain drawn back. She let it fall back into place as I passed by. Then I walked into my own house.

He was in the kitchen, sitting at the table, silent, alone. I didn't know what to say to him. Didn't know if I should sit with him. Put an arm around his shoulder. I thought I wanted to, but something else stopped me, some hidden force that made me feel any movement towards him would require a stepping outside of myself, and a passage through unsafe territory. I left him to his thoughts and went upstairs.

In my room I stared out through the window, at the calm warm night. I tried to make out patterns in the stars. At some point, I heard the roar of Kevin Ford's Honda escaping into the night. And I lay down in my bed, thought of Maria Cassidy's smile and waited for sleep.

The temperatures climbed higher and higher. More and more mothers started wearing bathing suits. Some of those already in bathing suits graduated into bikinis. While those in bikinis to begin with padded proudly up and down our road, their brown bodies glinting in the golden light. Even Mrs Redihan succumbed. She made a very bold move going straight from her cardigan into a bikini, by-passing the bathing suit stage. She had a very good body. So good that I thought she might give Maria Cassidy a run for her money. Someone is going to need to hear about this, I told myself, and at once I headed for Heff's house.

When I called for him he was busy scrambling his cube. He had broken the fifty seconds barrier and was talking about entering the national Rubik's cube contest.

'I am going to make a name for myself', he said, tossing his solved cube from one hand to the other. 'Then women will be throwing themselves at *me*'. He had also heard about Kevin Ford's party and the guards. 'It was Redihan who called them', he said. 'She really has it in for Ford'.

'Oh, I almost forgot', I said. 'She's in a bikini today. Redihan, I mean. She has a very good body. You should go take a look'.

On our way back towards Redihan's house, we passed Kevin Ford behind the steering wheel of his Honda, revving like he never had before. He was fuming. Mrs Cassidy was on her way back inside her house. I could tell she had just told Kevin Ford to take his Honda elsewhere. Heff and I walked on as he skidded away. A couple of seconds later we heard Kevin's car screech to a halt. When we turned around he was already out of his car, the driver's door was swung open and he was standing beside the bonnet of his car, his hands clasped behind his head. *Oh-oh*, I thought, *he's hit the dog*. Sure enough, Mrs Redihan appeared moments later. Then Maria Cassidy rushed past us, out onto the road. I looked after her. Then I heard Mrs Redihan's dog barking. It was moving swiftly down the grassy bank towards the scene. Ciara Cassidy was right behind. I looked from Ciara back to Kevin Ford's Honda.

Then I heard Maria Cassidy's scream, and I started to move closer.

He was lying on the road, not moving, blood was seeping out from the underside of his head. Maria slumped down on the road and with both arms gripped her boy and half-raised him off the ground. She was crying now, and little Stephen's blood was spreading across her brown skin, smearing her white bikini. Closer and closer to her she clutched her boy, as though doing so could somehow restore the precious little life. And the pain of that moment suddenly reached me. Waves of dizziness arrived, and I had to sit down on the curb before I fell. And I sat there and watched Mrs Cassidy cradle her lifeless boy, gently rock him back and forth. And I wanted her to hold me that way. I wanted to be her bleeding boy.

THE NIGHT MY SISTER ALMOST
FIXED ME UP WITH A PORN STAR

Jennifer is always trying to fix me up. 'Hello there', she says to many a bemused beauty. 'This is my only brother. He has poor coping skills but will make a considerate lover'.

I am not exactly sure what it is she is trying to accomplish with this provocative introduction. Nor, as far as I can make out, are her chosen targets for my selfless though flawed affections. 'There is no such thing as a considerate lover', a girl said back to her the other day. 'He is no good to me if he cannot cope', replied another. Neither reaction deters Jennifer from her romantic quest. Little is accomplished when I speak out against her methods.

'Daniel, you are grieving', she declares. 'You need a woman'.

'Jennifer, I don't *need* anything', I reply. 'Least of all love-advice from a celibate older sister'.

'Nobody knows what they need', she answers, with a petulant wave of her hands. 'But I know one thing. There is nothing nicer than a woman's body'.

Here we go again, I murmur to myself. As do other family members whenever Jennifer gets it inside her head precisely what it is any of us needs. We tend to tolerate Jennifer because she is the eldest, likes to spend her money and practises an extreme form of Tai Chi. Meantime, the rest of us mark our own lives according to some forever-fixed moment of personal crisis. The time I fell from a rooftop, for example, and smashed head-first through a pane of glass leaving me with a cross-shaped scar in the gap between my eyebrows. Or the time Frankie decided that she wanted to save Uganda and legged it without bothering to tell anyone. Or the time Lorraine announced to everyone that she was getting engaged to an eastern-philosophy student who liked to steal cars. Or the time the same sister announced that the engagement was off and that she was five months pregnant.

Not for Jennifer these life-is-stranger-than-fiction fiascos. Her rumble through life's jungle is a more modest affair. Putting herself behind people is her preference, and surrendering her own priorities to the wants of others. Jennifer parcels out her life in favours – keeping an eye out on my behalf, babysitting when Lorraine has a hot-date with the latest contemplative felon in her life, maintaining contact with faraway Frankie to ensure the runaway has adequate supplies of Cheese and Onion Taytos, Chef Brown Sauce and Oatfield Chocolate Emeralds – as though these little acts of worth represent the anchors Jennifer must reach for whenever she finds it all getting away from her. For Jennifer, affirmation arrives by way of her pocket book of good intentions – as opposed to the elaborate dramas orchestrated by her nearest and dearest. 'Someone has to be the lookout', is her claim in defence of her constant vigilance. This heightened sense of responsibility leaves her in a state of permanent unrest. She can never wait to be a good-doer.

'Sexually, I'm self-destructive', Jennifer says when I ask why she doesn't apply any of this finding-love assistance to herself. 'For me there is little hope', she continues after an intense moment or two – as though she has just sourced and accepted some higher judgement in the matter. 'I suppose I'm a bit like you', she concludes. 'I don't know how to translate grief into language that can be understood'.

'What grief?' I say back to her.

'There, there', she soothes, going at my back with her hand.

When it comes to finding my elusive maiden the music gig is Jennifer's preferred arena. Jennifer and I go to a lot of gigs together. Before life as an office girl, she worked in a record shop, and the shop manager still passes her the occasional complimentary CD. The shop manager loved Jennifer because she was so enthusiastic in her work. I used to think it was a fake enthusiasm, put on for effect, to reassure an uncertain country-&-western fan, to sway a dithering jazz-lover, to charmingly persuade the entire music-buying public that she had a special place in her heart for their favourite brand of music. 'I have to tell you, that is an excellent choice', she would say no matter what ridiculous music CD her customer was on the verge of purchasing. One morning, I was browsing in the music shop and I looked on in horror as she fell over herself to compliment a businessman wanting to buy for his wife a CD of *Roxette's Greatest Hits*. 'I can't believe you let that guy think he has taste in music', I said later. 'Everybody has taste', she threw back at me. 'Some like it with the merest touch of zest. Others prefer it lumpy and without meat. In the end it doesn't matter – we all end up in the same cooking pot'.

At tonight's gig *Goodtime Ray* has returned – by popular demand. I remember seeing him some time back. If memory serves, Goodtime Ray's idea of a good time is to sit on a low stool with his guitar and sing about the rain. Tonight, he begins his set with a number called *Persistent Drizzle*. 'I like this town', he caws in between his guitar chords. 'It reminds me of a sad story. Let me share my sad story with you beautiful people'.

Beside me, Jennifer is a finely-tuned antenna. Already she is scanning the venue, looking to pick out some ambivalent angel likely to inspire untapped reactions inside me. Soon, she ventures out on patrol. Returning to where I stand she reaches out to drag me.

'I think this could be the one', she says, hauling me across the crowded floor. 'I've had words. Found out a thing or two. Boys where this girl comes from are a lot like you. They're not territorial or physically capable. They have a vague sense of belonging. They do not acknowledge stop signs or seek comfort in late-night football. In her town she says that thanks to girls like her grieving is a thing of the past'.

I listen to this little speech and wonder what stop signs she is talking about. Also, I'm as willing as the next guy to watch football through the night – if Brazil is playing.

'Daniel, this is Carlene', Jennifer says when she finds who she is looking for. 'Carlene is from Portland. She speaks husky English. She has crossed the Atlantic to find a man. Carlene, this is Daniel. He has poor coping skills but will make a considerate lover'.

Her good work done, she then disappears.

The Portland girl is sucking a straw pointing out of an umbrella-cocktail. She is lean and sallow-skinned – athletic-looking – with straight sandy hair reaching half-way down her back. She is wearing a short denim skirt and an imposing black singlet with glittery writing. *Lazy Days*, the writing says. She also wears an ankle bracelet and a pair of Birkenstocks. Her toenails are painted to match the glittery writing.

'I knew of a tennis player called Carlene', I say. 'From Toronto. I think she once made it to round four at Wimbledon'.

'It's Carling not Carlene'.

'Your name is Carling?'

'Yes. The tennis player too'.

'As in the light-hearted lager?'

'I don't know if it's light-hearted. I don't drink it'.

'I hear it sells well in England. Carling, that is'.

'Never been there', she says.

'Portland', I say. 'That's in Canada, right'.

'Wrong. You don't often ask questions, do you?'

'You can ask a question if you like'.

'What is your porn-star name?'

'I beg your pardon'.

'I need to know your porn-star name. It's one of the ways I have of telling'.

'Telling what?'

'If we are meant to be together'.

Before I have a chance to respond, Goodtime Ray takes time out from his set to engage with his audience. 'I realised something when it rained', he caws, idly strumming his guitar. 'My girl no longer had the hots for me. Let's sing a song about the girl I lost'.

There is respectful applause as he launches into a burdensome number called *It's Raining In My Heart*. At first, it's just a localised shower. Soon, it becomes a torrential downpour. By the time the last chorus comes around the whole world is underwater. Throughout it all, however, Goodtime Ray can still glimpse the stars. 'How can he see the stars if it's raining all the time', someone calls out a little too loudly. 'I was in a great humour until he opened his mouth', says another.

'What do you think of the musician?' I ask Carling.

'He's like the weather', she answers. 'Goes from bad to worse'.

'He's a local musician', I say. 'He's been banging on about the rain for a long time. I don't think he's ever toured. I'm pretty sure he's never set foot outside this town'.

'This town is a lot like Portland', Carling says. 'The weather. The bridges. The vibe'.

'There is a good vibe', I say, like someone who has never before heard the word.

'All my stuff is in Portland', Carling says. 'My clothes. My records. I have a car in Portland. You should come. We have a chance of being together'.

'I don't know my porn-star name', I say.

'Yes you do', Carling says. 'Everybody has a porn-star name'.

'What's yours?' I ask.

'Fluffy Carty. I'm not crazy about it. But I'm stuck with it'.

'Why are you stuck with it?'

'It's how porn-star names work. You take the name of your first pet and combine it with your mother's maiden name. It's the golden rule with porn-star names. So I am Fluffy Carty'.

'I'm Rex Maguire', I say, after taking a moment to apply her special rule.

'Rex Maguire', she repeats after me. 'I like that. I like it a lot'.

'I think I like yours', I say back.

'Rex and Fluffy', she says. 'I think I can see a future for a couple called Rex and Fluffy. Are you really a considerate lover?'

'Only in my dreams. In reality I'm actually quite the lazybones', I reply, looking at the writing on her singlet. 'And I also have poor coping skills'.

'Where I come from I am considered extremely forbearing. I can help you cope'.

'It's looking good for us', I say.

'It is, isn't it', she says.

'What other ways have you of telling?'

Before Carling has a chance to answer, I am grabbed and hauled away. Jennifer shuffles me towards the exit door, glancing anxiously over her shoulder with every step she takes. 'I'm so sorry. I'm so sorry', she whispers in my ear as we move.

We reach the door and I turn back for one last glimpse of the Portland girl. But it is difficult to see through the bunching crowd. Steady but persistent handclapping is encouraging Goodtime Ray to do another song. 'I realised one last thing in the rain', he says to his devoted followers, plucking at his trusty companion. 'A guitar and a six-pack – that's all I need. This is my last song. It's called *I Hope It's Raining On The Day I Die*'.

'That was a narrow escape', Jennifer says, after she has dragged me around the corner from the music venue, all the time checking over her shoulder. 'I take back everything I said about that girl. She definitely is not the one to take you from your grieving'.

'What grieving?' I say back, throwing my arms into the cold night.

'There, there', Jennifer says, and she starts rubbing my back in slow circles.

The Good Crank

So many rushing into tomorrow. They cannot get there fast enough. Every man, woman, boy and child swerving from one moment to the next as though their lives depend on it. Slow down, I say. Take it easy.

'You've got to take the swift with the slow', Phyllis tells me. 'The eager with the meek'.

'I couldn't agree with you more, Phyllis', I say. 'I'll say hello to tomorrow when it arrives. But I've still got a little time for yesterday'.

These days I live on Single Street, the oldest street in our town. I'm one of two women living on this road. It's where we move to when our men run away or meet with an unfortunate end. When he had his chance my man chose to run. A JCB crushed Phyllis Quirke's. That happened in Australia. 'He wasn't taking any chances', she says. 'Ran away *and* met with an unfortunate end. He must have wanted shot of me bad'. Phyllis is my neighbour to the right.

Lifelong bachelors occupy the rest of our brittle road. Some are blind and some are deaf. So they go around in pairs. The deaf describe what they see – *oh look, Mattie, they've converted Rory Flint's abattoir into a fish museum*. The blind record all the gossip – *listen to this Tim, Gypsy Teresa says that if you change the past you can rearrange the future*. It's a very effective system. On a good day, any combination of them could run the country.

'You're a crank, Kitty Clog', Jack Lawless tells me.

'I know, Jack', I reply. 'But I'm a good crank'.

'How old are you today?' he asks.

'Six hundred and fifteen', I reply.

'The years have been kind', he says. 'You're now the second-best looking woman on this street'.

Jack has twenty-twenty vision and swears he can hear the stars. He grows herbs in his garden and lobs them into his pan of mince stew. When he has eaten his stew he claims he invented something called the iPod. 'Those little Japanese bastards get the credit for everything', he says, shaking his troubled head. He then wiggles through his herbs, a gadget the size of a breeze block clamped to his right ear. From time to time he pauses, raises a clenched fist and promises to visit hell-on-earth upon the Japanese. Jack is my neighbour to the left.

Though I'm old I still try to get about. I don't know where I'd be without my Raleigh Hybrid. It has eighteen different speeds and a pump suspension that allows me accelerate going through potholes. It's quite a pleasant feeling, actually. So I have put in a written request for more.

I do a lot of writing these days. It helps me get things off my chest. I set it all down on five-by-seven cards and address them to my runaway man. Cameroon, my Angolan postman, sees that they get there. He tells me he makes time for five-by-seven cards too. Except he uses images from *Time* magazine instead of words. Every Sunday he rows out into the bay, unloads his sack of cards and lets the tide take them. Healing balm for the soul he calls it.

When I write Hummer listens and corrects matters of grammar. She can sniff out a dud spelling before I've made it. She's always sniffing, poking her nose into business that doesn't concern her. I keep reminding her about what happened to the cat in the adage but it doesn't make any difference. She just loves collecting smells. She even describes them to me. 'Haddock', she screeches every Saturday morning. 'Branston Pickle', when Phyllis calls over. 'Marijuana', as soon as Jack surfaces.

'Whoopee', she yowled when my man ran. Hummer didn't like Henry. At least not after he introduced into our humble abode five Labradors, three Cocker Spaniels, two Golden Retrievers, and a Chihuahua called Pook. Hummer sniffed and ran every one of them. She ran Henry while she was at it. At least that's the theory I like to peddle. One day he was here – unravelling nets, varnishing oars, rigging up his boat – the next he was gone. Vanished. Just like that. *Away fishing* his note said. He didn't even thank me for the memories.

'You're a crank, Kitty Clog', Jack tells me.

'I know, Jack', I reply. 'But I'm a good crank'.

'Give me a kiss and I'll tell you what I've seen', he says.

'I'd rather lick an asp', I say.

Outside my window cement mixers chug and dumper trucks blunder their way through. Earth bashers pummel the field beyond my little garden. The developer promises to squeeze everyone in. Soon, there won't be room to swing a cat.

I consider taking it out on the time of year. Already, it's early autumn, the leaves are falling, and every day swallows congregate along rooftops and prepare to leave. It's seems like just yesterday they were back. 'Don't fall down', I hear a little boy call out as they fly. Often I wish I was among them, following the summer around the earth.

Hummer has her eye on the swallows too. 'Lunch', she snarls, but she may as well be yowling at the wind. Even that doesn't come easy. Not with all these earth bashers. *Thud-thud-thud*, they go. People have jobs, houses must be built I tell myself. Live and let live. Still. I catch myself praying for a purge. Meantime, bracts of thistle disappear and the yarrow sighs.

Sometimes I invite the developer inside for a cup of tea, a slice of currant cake. Before discovering property he tells me he was a Yoga Master. 'Finally I saw the light', he says, then mentions his plans to buy a peninsula in west Cork, build a submarine, the country's first indoor golf course and the largest nursing home there's ever been.

'May you live a thousand years', he says when I tell him I'll be his first customer.

'I'm already over half way', I answer.

'It must be hard to think clearly when you have no roof over your head', he says, gazing at my leaking tiles.

'Not nearly as hard as when you have too many', I reply.

'You're a crank, Kitty Clog', Jack tells me.

'I know, Jack', I reply, 'but I'm a good crank'.

'Dance a reel with me', he says, 'I'll spin you right around'.

'I'd rather go cheek-to-cheek with a tarantula', I tell him.

After my man ran I made friends with Notorious Reilly. Notorious used to be in the keeping-lonely-ladies-warm-on-a-cold-night business. In exchange for warmth I'd fry him a chop or two. 'Swine', yowls Hummer any time I mention Notorious.

Notorious kept Phyllis warm too. On balmy evenings we sit out the back and compare notes. One such evening Notorious hopped over the back wall.

'Hello girls', he said, with a twinkle in his eye.

'Will I stick on the frying pan, Notorious?' I asked him, winking at Phyllis.

'Not at all', he replied, winking back at the two of us. 'Tonight, I'm in the mood for a sandwich'.

It always amazed me how Notorious could lay his hat in so many places at the one time. Alas, now he lies in the new cemetery and Phyllis has become aware of her mortality.

'I'm never going to die', I calmly inform her.

'I used to think that way', Phyllis replies. 'Then I obtained expert opinion'.

And I hear all about the consultant. Handsome, with a pencil-line moustache. A dead ringer for Rhett Butler. Tell him your name, age, habits and history, and in thirty seconds he will give you your time and cause of death.

'I love his hands', Phyllis goes on. 'It only costs one hundred and eighty euros to shake them'.

'How much for an opinion?' I ask.

'You're a crank, Kitty Clog', Jack tells me.

'I know, Jack', I reply, 'but I'm a good crank'.

'Let's go to Fish Frenzy', he says, 'I'll shout you a Moby Dick'.

'I'd rather dine with the cannibals', I tell him.

Cameroon tells me he knows a charm that might improve my moods. Women where he comes from use it to bring back their vanished men. 'Give me something once cherished by your neglectful man', he instructs and I hand over the frying pan. Then begins an urgent summoning, a wailing plea that somehow reaches deep inside and wrenches out the icy shards within me, every sunken dream. 'Yikes', Hummer yowls when the frying pan takes to the air. 'No one has used the charm on me', Cameroon muses when his magic spell concludes.

Once alone, I sit up and keep watch. By the light of the moon I listen for the night's quiet declarations. Wayward thoughts find me. The fisherman's song. The frosts of wooing words gone cold.

Soon I hear a scratching at my window. Through the frosted glass I can even make out a ghostly form, an unresting spirit returned from some forbidding place with unfinished matters to attend. 'The magic is working', I gasp. 'It's my repentant man returned from his fishing'. Then the phantom speaks – a delicious devil-voice that tells me, in no uncertain terms, what it wouldn't do for one last chop.

Come morning the dumper trucks resume their rampant ways. After some rummaging, Phyllis presents me with a pair of ear plugs.

'What good are these', I say, kneading between my thumb and forefinger the two yellow bits of foam.

'You're dramatic', Phyllis says, stopping my restless hands. But she has now only one thing on her mind. 'Have you seen the cost of dying?' she remarks. 'It's obscene. I hope it happens to me soon. Otherwise I won't be able to afford it. I'm thinking of a green coffin. Do my bit for the environment'.

I plug my ears and pedal to the water. I taste the salty breeze and throw a fist against the ebbing tide. I scan the vacant horizon until I feel the cold. Until, at last, I begin to understand this corrupt murmuring inside my withered chest.

'How long have I got?' I ask the consultant when I'm carted into A&E.

'Your digestion has been mildly inhibited', he replies. Then he ladles out two mouthfuls of Gaviscon and refers me to a website. 'Euthymol toothpaste', yowls Hummer, when I offer her a saucer of my medicine.

Novembers are chilly in our town. Winter winds whistle. And the rains come on like furious applause. But I like the sounds of water. The waves at Silver Strand. The river's conversation with the stones. And when the temperature drops a little more, I like listening to the snow. There is much to be silent about. And there is always tomorrow.

Either side of me Phyllis has begun a funeral list and Jack rages into his breeze block. Outside they have laid a new stretch of road. 'There's a huge pothole in it', Phyllis says. 'Right outside your door'.

I ask the developer is his submarine ready yet. But he has changed his mind. 'Crematoriums', he bellows. 'I'm going to corner the market'. And there and then he unveils his fiery vision.

The deaf have started to wonder are their eyes deceiving them. The blind cling to the notion of changing the past to form the future. I can't quite get my head around this – after all, what's done is done. But if I could change one thing it would be this: I'd turn myself into a man. That way I wouldn't have to worry about my subdued appetite, this splintered heart inside me. And I could whine away in peace and quiet to my heart's content without that mince-frying herb-eater next door constantly banging on about what a crank I am. While I'm at it I might even turn Hummer into a Dobermann. I could train him up. And, maybe then, I could set about rearranging the future.

Beside Titan's Sea

When his parents were quarrelling and he was afraid to be around them Bernard went to his room and made use of whatever was there in order to distract himself. A bucket of Lego. His compendium of games. The cardboard castle used to house his collection of six hundred and thirty-seven marbles. It was all helpful.

Most helpful was his guide to the stars and planets. An uncle living in London had sent it to him for his ninth birthday. From it he transcribed pages and pages of information and statistics into the pad he had titled Astronomy. He drew charts indicating the positions of planets in relation to the sun. He listed out distances in light years it would take to reach famous stars. He loved mapping out constellations.

On clear nights he kneeled on his bed and looked out through the window in his room to scan the night sky for some of these constellations. He was pleased when he made out the Big Dipper also known as the Plough, Pegasus the flying horse, and Gemini the twins. He spent ages looking at the moon, and knew where Venus and

Mars were. Often he managed to find Orion, the constellation he had quickly decided was his favourite.

Later into the night, when he was lying in his bed, he heard the shouting in the second bedroom. It kept him awake and lasted until one of them gave up and pounded downstairs. In his bed he wrapped the pillow around his head and turned to face the wall. But it didn't do any good. He heard gasps, fragments of abuse, harsh words. He heard shuffling feet. Keys rattled. Doors opened and closed. Eventually, when it was quiet, he replaced the pillow beneath his head. Then he watched as the darkness started its tricks, and shadows moved along the wall.

In the morning he went outside and played by himself in the back yard. He had a football which he used to play out imaginary championships. He stroked a smaller ball against the yard wall with a tennis racquet. Sometimes he pumped more air into the football and added basketball to the list of games he played.

When he was tired he sat on the back doorstep or wandered to the end of the garden and leaned over the fence and looked up and down the back lane. If he was feeling extra adventurous he climbed over the fence and headed for the unfinished flats in the back field.

Though unfinished and abandoned, it was the highest building in the neighbourhood. To one side, the scaffolding was still intact, almost reaching the flat roof of the building. It had taken Bernard a long time to master his climb. After making it to each successive level, he had paused on the timber planks and found his balance before moving on. As he'd neared the top he had planted one foot onto the last of the scaffold poles, wedged his other foot into a cavity just below the roof and swung himself upwards for all he was worth. The day he had finally made it onto the roof, he stood looking around him. So high up was he, he had quickly become dizzy. But he had felt a sense of achievement upon scaling the lofty building and the following day he climbed again. And the next day. And the day after that. And again, until the climb came easily to him.

Once on top of the building he always sat down. That way he felt less dizzy. He sat in such a way that allowed his legs dangle over the edge. He sat there for hours, thinking and looking up at the sky and tracing the flight paths of jumbo jets that would frequently soar across the sky. He watched birds and wished he, too, could fly.

When he thought things would have calmed he climbed down off the building, crossed the back lane and stepped back inside the house. He had no idea of the time or how long he had been outside. By now, though, the patterns the quarrelling took were becoming a part of his day. Instinctively, he knew when it was a quiet time.

In his room he kept league tables for the games he played out in the yard. The football league was developing into a two horse race between Shamrock Rovers and Bohemians. Against all the odds, Ireland was doing very well in the European basketball championships. They had qualified out of their group into the knockout phase of the tournament where they would face England, their great rivals. Meantime, at the grand old age of forty-nine John McEnroe had come out of retirement and was exciting the crowds and commentators with thrilling displays as he progressed through the early rounds at Wimbledon. 'Ooh, I say', Dan Maskell remarked from the commentary box when McEnroe pulled off one of his trademark forehands.

Once the tables and round-robin charts had been updated, Bernard took out his guide to the stars and planets and copied another chapter into his astronomy pad. He wrote out the names of more constellations, worded the names of stars he liked the sound of, wondered how they came to be so called. Eventually, it was time for dinner and he had to go downstairs.

It was quiet at mealtimes. His father read the newspaper and looked stern. His mother stared at her food, perhaps asked Bernard some things about his day. What was he up to in his room? When was the next full moon due? Was he going to see David any time soon? Bernard sensed that she wasn't really interested in what he was up to. She just wanted to interrupt the silence, he thought. After a few questions his father tutted loudly, and pushed back his chair and took his paper and plate of food into the living room. His mother stopped talking and Bernard ate his meal as quickly as he could.

When he wanted a break from his room and wanted to get further away from the house, he called up to David. They had become friends just after the school holidays began. David lived at the top of the hill, in a triangular shaped house with his three aunts. 'They are so old they must have escaped from the graveyard', David told Bernard shortly after they had become friends. He called them the Terrible Sisters. A long time ago David had been adopted by the couple who ran the pub on Main Street downtown. But they didn't want David living in a pub, so he had been sent to live with the Terrible Sisters. 'They have lots of money', David also said. 'That's why they're let out of their graves'.

David knew lots of stuff about the stars. He had his own guide book, went spotting whenever he could and he showed Bernard his notebook where he wrote observations. He knew the names of the planets and their moons, and could list them in order of position from the sun. He knew where to find all the constellations. He knew the brightest star, the closest star and other important stars. He told Bernard about comets and asteroids and explained supernovas. He had a coloured chart that showed the positions of his favourite star clusters. He believed in UFO's. Since they had become friends Bernard loved stargazing more than anything.

When there was something to see, David threw stones at Bernard's window.

'Let's go spotting', he said, and Bernard left his room and joined his friend beneath the night sky.

'Show me Pegasus', Bernard asked, and David tilted his head and pointed. 'Show me the Water Serpent', Bernard said and David pointed again.

Then he picked out Jupiter and Sirius and a faint twinkling cluster that was very hard to see. 'The Pleiades', David said. 'The Pleiades are the seven screaming daughters of Atlas. And Atlas bears the world on his shoulders'.

'As if having seven screaming daughters isn't bad enough', Bernard said and David laughed.

'They're like my aunts', he said. 'You can't easily see them but they're always there'.

David loved spotting The Pleiades. But he didn't look straight at them. He turned his head or rolled his eyes into the corner of their sockets. 'Sometimes, the best things can only be seen out of the corner of the eye', he said.

'How many constellations are there?' Bernard asked.

'Who knows? Besides, the number is always increasing'.

'Have they all got names?'

'They're all named after The Gods. Long ago, they were put in the sky when they became a nuisance on Earth. In the sky they become immortal. They can never die. But they're always fighting with each other. Look at Mars up there. Mars is the God of War. He's red from all the blood he has spilled. He can fling thunderbolts across the universe'.

'Why are they always fighting?' Bernard asked.

'Because it's in their blood', David replied.

Orion was David's favourite constellation too. The Hunter, David called him. He made up stories about Orion. They were very far-fetched, but so were real stories, he said. 'When he finished hunting, Orion chased The Pleiades', David began. 'Then The Gods became fed up with Orion and his chasing. So they put him in the sky. Then they got fed up with the screaming Pleiades and put them in the sky too. Now Orion can hunt and chase all he likes. Look, you can see his belt, where he keeps his sword'.

The two boys spent hours sitting on the back fence of Bernard's house, gazing at Orion, waiting for him to do some hunting. Next door, Old Tom Crossan leaned on his walking cane and waited too, and the guitar player living the other side sang to the moon. Sometimes, Turnip Madden's horse reared up in the back field. And David would leap to the ground and pretend he was a swordsman. He rested one arm on his hip and thrashed away at the night with the other. 'Look, Bernard, they're attacking Orion', he called out when a shooting star appeared.

Bernard wanted to sit out all night listening to David. He wished he could've thought of more questions to ask. But eventually David went home and Bernard had to go inside.

At lunch time the following day his mother slammed the soup bowls down on the kitchen table so loudly his father glared out at her from behind his newspaper. Then his father pushed a bowl off the edge of the table, spilling soup all over the floor. Bernard stood up and reached for a cloth to wipe up the mess.

'Leave it', his mother shouted at him, and he did. Then she lifted up her own soup bowl and let it fall to the floor. The bowl smashed to pieces and more soup spread across the messy floor. His father kicked back his chair, sending it crashing against the kitchen wall. Bernard left the room and went outside.

He didn't know what they were arguing about. He wondered did his parents know. So long had they being going at each other it seemed to Bernard like one continuous argument. And that they no longer knew any other way to behave. As bad as the arguing was the period of silence that temporarily interrupted all the shouting. It wasn't an ordinary silence, Bernard thought, it was a silence that had fear and nervousness in it, and it travelled throughout the house, into every room, into every corner, upstairs and downstairs, there was no escape from it. It should have been a relief from all the shouting, Bernard thought. But it wasn't. It was merely an indicator of what was in store, a silent countdown. He was glad of the chance to call around for David.

The holidays progressed and the quarrelling worsened. In his room Bernard wrote in his astronomy pad and watched the shadows move along the wall. Outside in the yard he played out his championships. After that, he made his way as far as the back field and climbed onto the roof of the unfinished flats and sat with his feet hanging over the roof edge and stared into the sky and wondered what it was like in space. Then he called up to his friend's house at the top of the hill.

'Let's go spotting', Bernard said when David came to the door.

'It's not dark yet, you numpty', David said, laughing, and then invited Bernard inside his house.

David's house was quiet too. His aunts were nowhere to be seen, let alone heard. David padded through the place as though he had it entirely to himself. It was so silent, but it was different to the silence in his own house, Bernard thought. He felt safe.

'You're not going to believe this', David said as they stepped upstairs. 'The Terrible Sisters bought me a telescope'.

'Where is it?' Bernard asked.

'I knew you'd ask me that. Step this way'.

Bernard followed as David walked to one end of the upstairs landing and pulled down a collapsible stairs that led to the attic door.

'We have a converted attic', David said, starting to climb. 'It's where I do some of my best spotting. Come on'.

The telescope was resting on a stand and set up in such a way that it pointed through the Velux window in the converted attic.

'Here', said David, as he indicated to Bernard where he should best position himself.

'What's that?' Bernard asked, pointing to a poster taped up beside the window, an image of jagged rocks rising out of a sea of vapour

'That's the sea on Titan', said David, delighted to be asked. 'Titan is Saturn's largest moon. Look closer and you can see Saturn'.

Bernard stepped over to the poster and looked at it intensely. David was right. Through the thick orange atmosphere that dominated the top half of the poster you could make out Saturn and its rings and, further off, another of its moons, Bernard had no idea which one.

'Great, isn't it?' David said.

'Yes, it is'.

'It was taken by the *Huygens* space probe – when it landed beside Titan's sea. Do you know Titan's atmosphere-gravity ratio is so dense a human could fly across it – if he beat his arms fast enough? Imagine that'.

'What's it like in your house?' Bernard asked David next.

'This house or the one downtown?'

'The one downtown'.

'It's a mad house. My dad is mad. And my mother. I have an older brother too. You should hear him. He's the maddest of the lot of them. It never stops in that place. Especially downstairs – in the pub. They're always going mad in the pub. Guess what my brother did one night? He threw a punch at a customer in our pub. It's no wonder I'm sent to live here. What's it like in your house?'

'It's mad too. My mother is mad and my father. They're mad all the time. It never stops either'.

'You should stay over here some time. We can spend the entire night spotting'.

When he came home his mother was sitting on the back doorstep. She was wearing her coat and she had her knees bunched and her hands clasped around them.

'I was over in David's house', Bernard said. 'He has a telescope. We were looking at the stars'.

'Oh', she said, looking up at him, 'and what stars did you see?'

The question surprised him and, for a moment, he didn't know what to say. He mumbled some words, but gradually he started telling her about what he had been up to in David's attic room. He mentioned all the stars he'd seen and shared some of his new knowledge. He mentioned David's telescope and looking through it and what he'd seen. Then he mentioned the poster in David's room, and he started to describe Titan's sea and what David had said about its dense atmosphere, but when he looked at his mother he could tell she was no longer listening, and he stopped speaking and went inside.

Later, when he wasn't sleeping and he thought the shouting had stopped, he left his room and went downstairs. It was a clear night and he wanted to climb onto the roof of the unfinished flats for a closer look at the sky. But he didn't get very far. They were standing face to face in the kitchen, looking furiously at each other. He saw his father slap his mother's face. At once his mother slapped his father back. They started shouting again, glaring at each other like there was no tomorrow. He wished he had stayed over in David's house. He wished he could get away from this house for good.

'You'll never guess what my brother did', David said as soon as they had reached the attic room. 'He drank half a bottle of whiskey and wobbled around the house cursing and swearing like a drunk man. I didn't see it myself but I heard the Terrible Sisters talking about it. I told you it was a mad house. How's it going in your house?'

'It's looking like there'll be punches very soon. They slapped each other on the face after dinner last night. I was home just in time to see it'.

'Wow. Sounds like it's getting crazy in your house. And you got to see it'.

'Yeah, they were really mad'.

'*We* should do something mad', David said next.

'Tell me more about Titan', Bernard said. 'Tell me about its atmosphere'.

That night he thought about Titan and everything David had told him. Then he thought about what David had said about doing something mad. He thought long and hard about it, and it distracted him from all the shouting and shoving he could hear going on in the landing outside his door. But he couldn't come up with anything.

Later, it was so loud the pillow didn't do any good. 'I'm leaving, I really am!' he heard his mother scream when he sat up in the bed. Then it was quiet. He got out of bed, opened his room door and tiptoed downstairs. When he reached the bottom he looked down the hallway and saw his mother standing at the front door. She was dressed in her coat and hat, and she was carrying a suitcase.

'I'm leaving!' she screamed again.

He went back to his room. He took out his guide to the stars and planets. He hoped she would leave. Things would be different if she did. The shouting would stop, and the silence that came afterwards would have to find another angry house to infect. Some time later he heard footsteps on the landing. His bedroom door opened and his father walked in and sat down at the end of the bed. He stayed for a few minutes without saying anything, then left.

When he got up in the morning and went downstairs and saw his mother's coat hanging from the coat hook, he knew she hadn't left and his heart sank. In the kitchen he sat by himself, poking a spoon into his porridge. Then he pushed his breakfast bowl off the table. He watched as the milky porridge spread across the floor tiles, inching its way over the soup stains from before. He went outside and padded his tennis ball for a few minutes. He looked up and saw a jet cut across the sky. He wanted to get closer to it and he crossed into the back field and climbed up onto the roof of the unfinished building. He stood and tilted his head, and stared at the jet until he could no longer see it, until its trail of vapour had begun to dissolve. He stayed standing where he was and, though it made him dizzy, stood looking all around him, taking in the view afforded by the high building. He saw the spire of the cathedral and the railway bridge. He saw the school he went to. He saw the line of houses along the road he lived on. Then he saw his own house. He felt the silence and the atmosphere closing in on him. He spread out his arms like aeroplane wings. For a moment he veered from side to side. Then he realized he was favouring his left arm and he adjusted until he found equilibrium. He took a last look at the house he had come to dread. He stepped off the flat roof and started beating his arms.

BLOOMSDAY BUS DRIVER

When I was a young lad the sun used to shine all day on the sixteenth of June. Up it came at ten-to-five in the morning and didn't disappear until twenty-past-ten that night. We lived five miles from the sea and one Bloomsday morning my mother gave me a pound and said, 'Off with you now, go get a tan and figure out your life'. So I made my way to the station, gave the pound to the bus driver, sat in behind him and stared out at the clear blue sky.

The thing was everybody knew about the sun coming out on the sixteenth of June, and so the bus had to stop every twenty-five feet or so to pick up another passenger bound for the shimmering waters. By my steadily improving mathematical calculations that meant the bus was going to stop more than a thousand times before reaching the sea. I was glad I had inherited my father's knack for patience.

To help distract everyone from the start-stop nature of the journey the bus driver provided a running commentary. 'It's a great day to be alive', he said as people clambered aboard. 'I wish I had the day off myself', he offered as he punched holes in tickets. 'You are lucky, lucky people', he declared as he eased the bus back into motion.

About four hours into our journey, with over half of the five-mile trip already behind us, the driver stopped the bus even though nobody had flagged it down.

'I'll be back in a second', he said, climbing out of his seat. 'I want to ask that foxy lady a question'.

She was leaning against a wall, licking an ice-cream cone. Some ice-cream was smeared across her top lip. She was wearing a white dress, and every few seconds some wind reached in off the close-by sea and lifted the dress a few inches above her knees. The bus driver leaned against the wall beside her. He plucked a long stem of reed-grass and started chewing on it. After a moment he pointed to the ice-cream cone. The lady passed it over, and he ditched his reed and took a gob-full. When the ice-cream was gone the lady jerked a thumb over her shoulder. Then the two of them disappeared inside the house set back off the road. We all stared out to see what was happening. Some passengers became worried.

'I need to get some sun today', said one fretful lady. 'I'll die if I don't'.

'Yes, but how are we going to get to the beach?' said another. 'That lad is very distracted'.

'Does anyone know how to drive a bus?'

I wished I could've said, 'I do'.

Instead, one or two older men took it upon themselves to replace the absent bus driver. They strode purposefully through the aisle of the bus, one with a poor excuse for a moustache growing above his lip, the other wearing a straw hat and a jacket with stripes. The man trying to grow a moustache winked as he passed the worried ladies, as if to say, don't panic girls, I'll have us on the way to the sun in a jiffy. But when he and his accomplice reached the driver's seat they realised the bus man had taken the keys with him. At once they threw their arms into the air, turned to their expectant crew members with a look of helplessness and the fretting started all over again.

'Look', someone to the back of the bus spoke out, with traces of fear entering his voice. 'The sun is starting to go down'.

'I'm going to die', the fretful lady said. 'I really am'.

There wasn't much talking after that. Everyone sat back into their seat, sighing at the fading sun and at the sombre shadow gradually enveloping the countryside. Then we spotted the bus driver. He was rushing down the pathway of the house he had been inside, tugging his shirt back into his halfway-down trousers. His hair was tossed and one of his shoes was missing. As soon as he climbed into his seat he was in no mood to hang about.

'I'll drive you all home personally', he said, and one or two women raised their eyebrows.

'That was one reluctant bus driver', said the lady who thought she was going to die when we pulled up at my stop.

'Young lad', he said as I stepped off, and he flipped a coin at me. At once I made a dash for Mel Campbell's paper shop, he always stayed open late.

'I'll have an ice-cream cone', I said to the girl behind the counter. 'One with a Flake in it'.

She took a cone from the stack beside the ice-cream machine, pulled the lever and, once she could pile on no more, offered me the towering sculpture along with a smile that, in times to come, would make the wind blow across my soul. It was more or less dark when I stepped inside the kitchen of our house.

'That's not much of a tan', my mother said when she looked up from her paper.

'No', I agreed, 'but when I'm big, I'm going to be a bus driver'.

WALKING AMONG RUINS IN BABYLON

'Help', said the person at the end of the line. 'There is blood everywhere'.

'Right', I said. I was still more or less asleep.

'Do you hear me?' came the voice. 'I am sitting in a pool of blood'.

'I think you have the wrong number', I said.

'For God's sake', the voice said to me. Then the line went dead.

'Who was it?' Marian asked as soon as I set down the phone on the bedside locker.

'I'm not sure. I think it was a crackpot', I said, sitting up a little in the bed.

'A crackpot? What's a crackpot doing ringing us?'

'I'm not sure. Something about blood. It sounded like there was lots of blood'.

'What? Whose blood? I don't like the sound of this'.

'Me neither. I'm fairly sure it was a crackpot'.

We looked at each other, and as soon as we did, the phone started ringing again.

'Jesus Christ!' said Marian.

'I'm not answering it', I said.

'Answer it, for God's sake!' Marian said, just like the caller had, and I leaned over and lifted the phone.

'You've got to help me!' the voice said.

'That's enough out of you!' I said and hung up.

We both sat up in the bed. Marian had one hand covering part of her face. I was frowning at the phone.

'One of these days we need to think about changing our phone number. Or going ex-directory. Or getting rid of the phone', Marian said.

'We hardly ever use it any more', I said, rubbing my eyes.

'Exactly', Marian said.

'The only time we use it is to answer somebody calling us at four o'clock in the morning'.

'That's right', Marian said.

'I can throw it away right now if you want', I said, but Marian didn't reply to that. Instead she removed the pillow from around her head, bunched it up and placed it lengthways behind her back, against the headboard.

'Is it really four o'clock?' she asked.

'Yes it is', I said, glancing at the digital clock.

'Four o'clock. Jesus! I have to be up in three-and-a-half hours'.

'Well, let's snuggle down again', I said. 'If we're lucky we can get right back to sleep. No harm done'.

'Did you not hear what I said? I have to get up soon. I can't go back to sleep now'.

'I did hear you. But I don't see how it should interfere with the few sleeping hours available to us'.

'What if the person rings back? What if I have just slipped back into a dreamy sleep and the phone goes off again?'

'Do you want me to put it on silent?' I asked.

'It doesn't matter. I'm awake now. I don't think I'll go back to sleep. I think I'll have a cup of coffee. You could make it for me?'

'I don't want to make coffee', I said. 'I want to go back to sleep'.

'Fine. I'll get it myself'.

But she didn't move. She just sat up a little more, puffed up her pillow again, reached over to her side and switched on the lamp. Then she reached for her nail file and started stroking her nails.

'I wonder who it could have been?' Marian said, as she moved the file across her nails.

'Who knows?' I said. 'At least it wasn't your mother!'

'What was that?'

'Your mother', I repeated. 'It could have been her on the phone. I'm saying it wasn't her, thankfully'.

'Leave my mother alone. She isn't well'.

'Exactly, and all I'm saying is it could have been her calling, or someone calling on her behalf. You know, to say that there is a problem – maybe. But it wasn't like that. It was only some nut job out there in the world, somewhere, with nothing better to do than bother people with prank calls. I wasn't trying to sound uncaring. OK?'

'You know I get a little spooked when the phone goes off in the night', Marian said.

'I thought you were going to get some coffee', I said, deciding it best to rewind the last moment or so, and, to my surprise, Marian set down her nail file, whipped off the duvet, swung herself out of the bed and felt about the floor for her slippers. Only she didn't make her way downstairs. She didn't even leave the bedroom. She headed for the bathroom, the ensuite, and closed the door behind her. I started to have a bad feeling about getting back to sleep, and I was sorry I had dragged Marian's mother into it.

She was an old lady now, more or less immobile, and, thanks to the millions of cigarettes she'd smoked throughout her long life, her lungs had just about given up the ghost. There was a good chance she was starting to lose her mind too. Not two days ago we'd visited her at the nursing home and she'd thought I was her long dead husband. 'Barry, could you make me a hot water bottle?' she had kept saying to me. At first I'd thought she was trying to wind me up – she knows well my name is Paul, not Barry. Then it became apparent that something *was* going on with her mind, something really heartbreaking. 'Barry, could I borrow a cigarette off you?' she asked me, even though I haven't smoked in years. 'Barry, could I trouble you for a light? Barry, remember the time we went to see Johnny Cash? Barry, I want you to hold me', she said, making room beside her in the bed.

She did not let up for the entire duration of our visit. Marian even asked me to play along, which I was happy to do – I was feeling sorry for her – but as soon as that *hold me* request came my way, I thought it might be time to play a different game. 'What is all this about?' I asked Marian when I thought her mother had gone to sleep, but my wife just put her finger to her lips and sent me off for a packet of Majors.

Most days she was fine, the carers had told us some time ago. She knew exactly who was who, and where she was, and what the rest of us were all at. She would ask for us on these days, even go so far as to ask one of the carers if she could put a call through to our house so that she could speak with her daughter. That's why Marian bought the mobile. It was one of many gestures she thought might make life a little easier for her mother. The mobile had large buttons and Marian spent an afternoon showing her mother how to make a call by pressing just a couple of these buttons. And so, from time to time, her mother would think of the mobile and make a call to our house.

Usually she called to ask Marian to come and see her. And to bring her something: a blanket she had a particular fondness for, some fresh flowers, certain newspapers she had gotten it inside her head that she would like to read. Marian was only too happy to oblige. She was glad she could help her fading mother, glad to have this time with her so close to the end.

Soon, the calls were coming through at any time. Early on a weekend morning. During the course of a busy work day. Right smack in the middle of the night. And, once she'd gotten it inside her head to make a call, Marian's mother wouldn't let up until someone had answered. In next to no time, it seemed, she was constantly jabbing the mobile's buttons, had figured out its system of short cuts, was becoming very fond of the redial button. Her quick ability to use it and desire to do so at any time, it seemed to me, had given her a new lease of life. I said as much to Marian in our kitchen one evening. And just then, as if by way of confirmation, our landline went off and Marian had to skip dinner and make a trip in to her mother.

The upshot of it all was that Marian was in big demand. Her mother would call with her inventory of requirements and Marian would drop what she was doing and make a trip downtown to hunt for what was needed. In no time her mother's room had become cluttered with an assortment of items. Rugged slippers to withstand the nursing home's shiny floors. Boxes of Jaffa Cakes to spice up the nursing home's unending supply of Rich Tea biscuits. A locker full of remedies to combat, at various times, barbaric doses of heartburn, constipation and other unannounced discomforts.

By and large, Marian had no problem with these calls. Neither did I. Who wouldn't want to help out an old lady in distress? But sometimes she called up for no obvious reason, and at a bad time. Once recently, into the early hours of a Monday morning, Marian hadn't answered the phone – she hadn't been able to because she was exhausted after having had to work through the weekend nights, she'd been on call. Her mother had become really upset at the nursing home, so much so that Marian had had to take the Monday off work and spend it trying to placate her and reassure her that she would always be at the end of the phone. 'I depend on you', her mother said many hours later, when Marian had finally managed to subdue her mother's anxiety.

'I could do with a break', Marian said the Sunday evening after. She had spent the entire weekend running errands for her mother and was not looking forward to the work week ahead of her. 'Well then, let's go somewhere', I said. 'OK', said Marian and we made plans to get out of town the following weekend. We received a blessing from Marian's mother too. 'Have a wonderful time, bring me back something nice', she said to us. We nearly even made it. We were only about ten miles from our destination when the call came through. I could hear her cackling away inside Marian's mobile, slowly starting in on whatever it was that was bothering her, and before the conversation had ended I was swinging the car around for the journey home.

During the drive back, I suggested to Marian that she should let her sister Imelda know what was happening with their mother, maybe Imelda could consider coming home for a visit? That way she too could have some time with her mother. Maybe the two of you could work out a sort of timetable I said to Marian, take turns visiting? But Marian reminded me about the time she had once before tried suggesting such an arrangement to her sister and, in particular, the response her suggestion had received. I thought better of pushing on with my idea, and so held my peace.

'I'm afraid', Marian's mother said to us at the nursing home. 'Afraid of what?' I was going to ask her, but it was late and I was tired and disappointed that we hadn't got away, and I was afraid myself that if I did open my mouth I wouldn't be very pleasant, and so I didn't say anything. Later again that night, in between answering three more phone calls, one of which was a request for a set of nail clippers, I had a dream I was strangling Marian's mother.

I heard the toilet flush, and a moment later Marian stepped out of the ensuite. She padded around the room, kicked off her slippers and got back under the covers.

'Are you coming with me in the morning?' Marian asked, resuming her finger work with the nail file.

'I can't', I said. 'I have some work to finish for Monday'.

'You always say that'.

'That's because it's true'.

'It's nothing that can't wait'.

I didn't say anything to that. And we were both silent for a moment or two. During the silence I considered reminding Marian about accompanying her to see her mother a couple of days ago, and how I had spent much of last weekend at the nursing home, and had given up lots of work time on several other occasions in the not too distant past. I was about to voice my thoughts, but one or two recently misworded and badly thought-out protestations came into my mind, and so I said nothing. Instead my thoughts turned to the coffee she had been talking about making, and how I was warming to the idea after all. Now there was a tension in the air, however, an unwelcome atmosphere in the room, something that should never have been let out.

Next thing the phone started ringing again. It was enough to make Marian jump. My own heart leapt a bit at that. I was sorry I hadn't silenced the thing.

'Are you going to answer it?' Marian said.

'OK', I said a little too quickly, and I snatched up the phone.

'Help me!' the voice said straight away. It was the same voice as before. 'Quickly, before it's too late!'

'Get lost!' I said loudly into the receiver and let the phone fall out of my hand. It landed on the floor with a dull thud. I leaned over as though I needed to see what the phone was now up to, then I dragged the bed clothes up around my chest. All the time, Marian was looking at me, as though I should be behaving in a more grown-up way.

'Well?'

'It's the nut job again', I said. 'They really have it in for us tonight'.

'What did they say?'

'They just keep asking for help and say that time is running out'.

'What sort of help? What do they sound like? Who is ringing us? Will you please start making sense, I'm getting a little freaked out!'

'It's nothing', I said, 'please don't worry. Obviously someone has got our number and is determined to have some fun at our expense. Whoever it is will soon get tired of their little game. So don't worry. OK. Look on the bright side, it could have been your sister. At least it wasn't her'.

'What the hell is that supposed to mean?'

When I gave no answer she whipped off the duvet and sat out of the bed. She stretched her arms, stood up, and walked to the wardrobe and reached for her nightgown. In the dim light she felt about for her slippers. Then she padded out of the room. By now, I was fairly certain I wasn't going to get back to sleep.

It was true, though. If it wasn't Marian's mother calling us up for no obvious reason, chances are it would be her sister Imelda calling with some crazy experience in her life she wanted to spend ages talking to Marian about and then ask for advice she had no intention of heeding. These calls could arrive at any time too, because Imelda was living in Africa or South America – I wasn't sure where, she was always on the move – anyway somewhere remote and poor, where there were no clocks, and so she never knew what time it was when she called. The call usually arrived via an operator who would first of all ask could we accept a reverse charge call at some crazy rate per second. 'Of course I'll take the call', Marian would say, and wait for her sister's voice.

Often she called when she needed something she didn't know how to get hold of herself. So far this year we had posted off a multi-bandwidth transistor, a digital camera, a three-tier Swiss army knife with a built-in altimeter, a compass, mosquito netting, malaria tablets, a second digital camera after the first one was stolen, two sets of binoculars, three sacks of cheese and onion flavoured Taytos and a tent. 'Can she not get any of this stuff herself?' I had asked when we were shopping for the tent, and I received a look that would have sent shudders through a giant oak.

We were supposed to go and visit her when she first moved away to Africa. But she wasn't a month gone out of the country when she was calling up with instructions for us not to make any hasty plans. 'I don't want anybody interfering with my settling in', she said when Marian asked why not. 'I will let you know when I'm ready for visitors', she told her sister. That was seven or eight years ago.

I'm not sure what exactly she has been up to since. Over time she had hauled herself from one continent to the next, involved herself in various do-good projects, snippets of which she told us about whenever she put through one of her urgent-request calls. One time we got a postcard from Somalia. There was a picture of a circle of men sitting around a smoking stone. One or two of the men were holding long pipes to their mouths. 'Look how colourful everything is', Marian said and stuck the postcard to the fridge with the aid of a Buddha magnet that had previously arrived from somewhere in India. Later, though, I pulled the postcard off the fridge and took another look at it. What's so colourful about it, I wondered. Then I wondered what Imelda was up to in Somalia.

She was supposed to come home at Christmas a couple of years ago. We drove up to the airport to welcome her home. So as to quickly spot her sister wheeling her luggage through, Marian took up position in front of the arrival gates. That way, upon spotting her, she could let out a big whoop and rush through the waiting crowd and throw her arms around her sister. 'I want to hear everything', Marian practised asking her sister on the drive to the airport. 'I can't wait to hear what she has been up to', she said to me in the car. If she said it once, she said it a hundred times.

Imelda never made it that Christmas. We waited four hours at the airport, maybe seven. It turned out she'd had to change her plans. 'A last minute crisis', Imelda told Marion a couple of days later, among other things, when the call explaining her no-show had finally come through. She couldn't make it the following Christmas either. Or the one after that – last Christmas. By then, she was busy helping forest-clearers and seed-planters in central Africa. That's what she'd said when that call came through. By then, you could also add a pair of adjustable walking boots, two night-lights and a gas cooking kit to the list of requests for the post bag, as well as various pills to help ease constipation and diarrhoea, which essentially meant tossing extra boxes into the trolley when out shopping for Marian's mother. She'd even asked for a batch of axe handles to be sent out. 'Why don't we just show up and clear the forest for her?' I said to Marian, and was I sorry.

Then she became some sort of freedom fighter. She was on World Report on the radio talking about the hell on earth innocent people were going through. Some eejit in Dublin wrote an article about her in the paper. I couldn't understand a word of it. Even the Six O'Clock News mentioned her. I couldn't believe it when I arrived in from work and saw her being interviewed by Sharon Ní Bheoláin. Marion was glued to her chair and waving me into the room and gesturing with her fingers, first on her lips for me not to say a word, then pointing to the television which she had cranked to full volume.

'What is the current situation over there, Imelda?' I heard Sharon Ní Bheoláin ask, and then the television camera was pointing at Imelda who was wrapped up in a white sheet and standing beside a camel. Then she was off into a long lecture about human rights and abuse and narrow escapes in the desert. Next thing she was dragging another freedom fighter into the camera shot. He was very tall and lean and his black skin was glistening and, as he fidgeted with the bandoliers that criss-crossed his torso, Imelda was introducing him to the world as the bravest, most noble man on earth. She couldn't keep her eyes off him. Sure enough, when the call came through, she was telling Marian all about the new love of her life. 'How was I on television?' she began, and got quickly into freedom talk and the hero in her life. Then she asked if Marian could send out another pair of boots and more Taytos. 'Are they for the camel or the freedom fighter?' I asked and Marian almost sliced me open with the look she gave me.

Late one night not so long ago she called – via the reverse charge operator – and I picked up the phone. 'Marian is at the nursing home', I told Imelda. 'Is there anything I can do?'

'Well, Paul, the way I see it the only thing you have to do is look after Marian. Make sure she is happy. Give her a little something every once in a while. Bring joy into her life'. She went on like that for a few minutes and I had to remind myself that she was living in a different time zone to the rest of us and that it would be impossible for me to strangle her there and then.

I took another look at that postcard with the smoking stone and wondered some more about Imelda's unconventional career path. Purifying water. Eradicating cholera. Chopping down a forest to plant seeds. Fighting for freedom. I didn't know. When she got back from the nursing home, Marian didn't seem to know either. It was a mystery. Think of all that she has given up, was all Marian had to say. Think of all the suffering people she is helping. And so, once again, I tried my best not to say what I really thought.

'I wouldn't mind, but I was in the middle of a great dream', Marian said. She was back in the bedroom, under the covers, yawning a bit. 'I was really enjoying myself – if you know what I mean'.

'I think I was dreaming too', I said. 'But I can never remember them anymore – unless they're upsetting or contain scenes of violence'.

'Like the one about strangling my mother?'

'Did I tell you about that? I don't remember. Jesus! I must be losing it'.

'You're getting old, that's all'.

'Sometimes I wake up and I know I've been dreaming. I can almost reach out and touch it. Then, just like that, it's gone. I used to have a great memory. I was proud of my memory. I can still remember things I did when I was a boy. I can remember details and all the names involved and the places and colours. And my dreams. I can remember dreams I had when I was a boy. Some of them must be over forty years old at this stage. Think of it. Tell me about your dream'.

But Marian didn't answer. I looked over and saw that she had fallen asleep. I'd been waffling on about fading memory and getting in touch with the distant past and showing off my childhood stories, and Marian had fallen asleep listening to me. I looked again, and closely. She *had* fallen asleep. After all her talk about coffee and having to get up soon and everything she had to do, she had fallen asleep. I wasn't surprised, though. She'd been working hard recently at the accommodation complex she managed, putting in long evenings, too many if you ask me, and weekends too. I reached over and, as delicately as I could manage it, removed a strand of hair that was inching its way towards the tip of her nose. She murmured at my touch, but she didn't wake up. I smiled and watched her for a minute. You're exhausted, I thought.

It made me think of another recent addition to the night callers. Marian's boss. How could I have forgotten about him? As soon as I'm finished strangling Marian's sister I'm going to start in on this joker. He's a developer and his idea of doing business was spending lots of time getting friendly with old people before they died. Before he made friends with them he made sure that they owned something – like forty or fifty acres of undeveloped land – and that they had nobody to leave it to when they died.

No building contractor was too cheap for this joker. No tradesman too unqualified. No security firm too sloppy. Marian had been working for him for seven years before he started calling her up in the middle of the night. In that time she had progressed from life as a wages clerk to manager of an accommodation complex near the university. The Village it was called. All year long The Village was full of students, and never a week passed without some idiotic incident that required Marian dropping everything and offering immediate assistance.

The cameras are down. Marian, can you go in and take a look? The guards have caught someone breaking into the convenience shop. Marian, can you go in and assist with the details? There's a fire in one of the apartments. Marian, can you go in and see if it's under control? These are some of the things Marian's joker boss had said upon calling in the middle of the night. Why can't you go in, joker? I felt like telling him the last time he called. I was all set to, but Marian grabbed the phone off me and listened to his sorry voice telling her the coin machine for the laundry had stopped working and asking if could she go in.

One night I had to get up and drive her in. She'd had a couple of glasses of red wine to calm herself down after receiving two other calls, one from her mother who had called up in a terrible state because Marian hadn't been in to see her in two days – you could hear her mother's tears spurting out of the phone at our end, she was that upset, and the second from her sister pleading for some quick cash to be wired to somewhere in Afghanistan or Turkmenistan – I don't know, one of those places that ends in Stan – because she had been mugged and needed to catch a fast plane. Anyway, whatever the crazy details were, by the time her boss phoned in his request Marian had had some wine and was afraid she would be over the limit. 'Who'll be out checking at this time of night?' I said to her, trying my best not to wake up. But out of bed I got, like a fool, and across town and over the misting bridge as far as her work place I drove her, like a fool, and damn it if all hell wasn't breaking loose at The Village.

At first, it looked like some sort of fancy dress-up party. Youngsters, hoards of them, dressed up as superheroes. Only they weren't the kinds of superheroes who went around rescuing the world. They were the kinds of superheroes hell bent on causing as much destruction as possible. I spotted Spiderman pelting paint bombs at car windows. Batman and Robin were trying to set a skip full of rubbish on fire. Iron Man was standing on top of the abandoned security hut, simultaneously swigging from a flagon of cider and relieving himself. Then, out of the mist, appeared a lad with several layers of toilet rolls wrapped around his body with masking tape. He was carrying something that looked like a car battery and he ran towards a bunch of youngsters, stopped when he was among them, pressed a button on the battery he was carrying and let out an almighty roar. All at once the bunch of youngsters dropped to the ground. Some of them lay on the ground, as still as corpses. Others started shaking arms and jerking their legs and other parts of themselves. Meantime, the lad with the toilet rolls strapped to his body was running towards another bunch of youngsters, and when he reached them the exact same thing happened all over again. 'Who is he supposed to be?' I asked Marian. 'I think he's a suicide bomber', she replied and we both looked at each other and we laughed. Then I drove us the hell out of there.

Her mother. Her sister. And her boss. That was three people right there, a cocktail strong enough to hammer anyone into the ground. And that's before I got started in on our son. I hadn't mentioned him before because every time I did I wanted to strangle him. I really did. I know he's my son, and I often think of all the fun we used to have when he was very young, times we would go hunting together for horse chestnuts or mushrooms, and go down to the courts and shoot baskets, and later at night, as best I could, answer his questions about stars. Right now though, I could wring his neck.

Ben. More than anyone it was Ben who kept Marian up nights. He was the biggest reason she always answered the phone in the night; he was the reason the phone was never disconnected. It was Ben she was holding out for. The funny thing was though, of all the people calling up looking for Marian to cancel her going away plans or to send fast cash three-quarters way around the world or to get out of bed at three o'clock in the morning in order to help some eejit insert a coin into a washing machine, our son was the one person who never called.

I never brought him up unless I had to. Mention of his name upset Marian. The rest of them could throw what they liked at her. But our son – that was where she was vulnerable. He was the one person she'd have loved to get a call from. Any time. Morning, noon or night. She'd have loved a call from him in the middle of the night. She'd have loved if the nut job out there who kept bothering us was our son. My luck ran out the day I lost my boy, she often said. The first time I heard that I thought she was being theatrical, a little bit over the top. He's giddy, I'd said. Let him go see some of the world. But as time passed, and we'd hear little then nothing about what our boy was up to or where in the world he was or if he was planning to come home, it would cut me up when I'd hear her say it.

To tell the truth, it broke my heart. Made me feel useless. And that I'd done a bad job with him. And if I could've made it happen, I'd have grabbed our son by the ear, hauled him to the nearest pay phone or internet café and had him make a call to his mother. I'd have had him calling every minute of the day if I'd thought it would cheer Marian up a little. I'd pay for the calls myself, wouldn't care where they came from, at what time of day, how long they lasted. He could be calling for any reason, to ask for the price of a ticket to Tahiti or for the loan of a VISA card – here, keep the thing I'd say to him. Or he could call for no reason at all. He could call, say hello mum, hello dad, and we'd take it from there – anything to hear his voice. Marian had even gone to the trouble of buying a laptop computer, setting up an email account for herself, and finding out everything there was to know about Skype. But most of the time her email box was empty, and she never got to wear her Skype headset. One call, was it too much to ask of someone?

He turned twenty-two on his last birthday. Or was it twenty-three? If it was, that made me exactly twice his age. Time flies. Anyway. By now he'd been travelling for well over two years, no doubt been to lots of places, had sent us the odd postcard, every one of which Marian had spent days staring at. 'I'm on my own personal journey, dad', he'd said to me setting off all those months ago, carrying little more than a sleeping bag and a pen. Last we'd heard from him was a two-line email letting us know he was on his way to visit Imelda somewhere in Nepal. Good luck to you there, son.

I looked over at her again. She was fast asleep. Dreaming about something or someone, perhaps. Her mother. Work. Our son. Who knew? She was wheezing too, not so gently either, and I knew she had fallen into a deep sleep. To be honest I was amazed she didn't fall asleep more often and not wake up for a month.

But one night her mother rang and Marian didn't wake up. She slept right through the ringing telephone. So I answered the phone and I heard this cackly old voice. 'Hello', the voice said. 'Imelda, is that you? Imelda, are you listening to me? I just wanted to call and say thank you for everything you're doing for me and for being there every time I've needed you. I don't know where I'd be if it wasn't for you, Imelda. I just wanted to call and tell you that'.

I thought she was going to hang up then but she didn't. I could hear her breathing down the line. She sounded hoarse and wheezy, and I was sure she had forgotten she was on the phone. Then she spoke some more. 'I'm afraid', she said, sounding suddenly very frail. 'I'm afraid of something and I don't know what it is'. Then she hung up.

I hadn't said a word to any of this. I'd just let her wheeze away for the few minutes and when I thought she was finished I put down the phone and lay back down into the bed. But after that call I hadn't been able to get back to sleep. I couldn't stop thinking about what she had said about being afraid, and I felt sorry for her being so old and having to face something, not knowing what it was. And, for a moment, I thought I could sense the fear she had been going on about all this time, and I lay there feeling bad that I had lost my patience once or twice recently. I turned over then and I spent the rest of the night staring at my sleeping wife – just like I was doing right now.

I never told Marian about her mother calling to say thanks. She would have wanted me to rehash everything that was said, word for word, as though it was a coded request for something her mother wanted, and I didn't want to get into any of that. I would have had to mention about the mother getting her daughters' names mixed up, and though it was now a normal mistake for the old lady to make, I didn't want Marian knowing her mother had called her by that other one's name. I could have tried to fib my way through it, but past form let me know I'd have cocked it up and then Marian would see I was trying to cover up something and that would end up making a bigger deal of it than it was and it would all end at the same result – with an upset Marian. And I didn't want to have to report her mother's words about being afraid and not knowing why. That would've spooked Marian and I thought it would be a good idea to spare her that. And so I kept it from her.

It was almost light outside. I looked over at Marian. She looked peaceful, and I was both happy and sorry for her. Happy because she was getting some shut-eye. Sorry because I knew she had a stressful day ahead of her. And right then I wanted to tell her a few things. I wanted to tell her how I thought she was a good daughter to her ailing mother, a good sister and a good mother. I wanted to tell her how I thought she was a good wife to me, a great friend, at times, an unforgettable lover. I wanted to tell her how I thought she still looked good to me, especially in those faded Levis she thought were too small for her. I really wanted to tell her all these things, but she was asleep now and I didn't have the heart to wake her. Her alarm would take care of that in little over an hour's time.

Instead, I thought about writing her a little note and leaving it by the bread basket I suddenly thought about setting up for her downstairs. A breakfast treat to send her on her way. I thought about some more things I could do for her. Take her out for a meal at the weekend. Buy her flowers. Maybe catch a show. Then I thought about booking us a weekend away some place and this time going through with it. Some place far away even, like Paris or Rome. A city break, staying in one of those boutique hotels. I was thinking about all this and getting really excited and starting to feel full of possibilities, and I was plotting further and further down the line, and everything was starting to look rosy again, and even though Marian had dragged my share of the duvet across her side of the bed, a warm feeling was travelling through me, I mean all the way through me, and for once I didn't mind that I hadn't slept and that I wouldn't get much work done that day.

I was thinking about all this, about where we were going to go and the room we would be staying in and what we would be doing in it, and it wouldn't matter if Marian's mother called us or her sister or her boss, it wouldn't matter at what time of day or night they were calling us, and whatever they wanted would have to wait because Marian and me would be far away, far away in Egypt worshipping the pyramids or walking among ruins in Babylon or floating up the Limpopo River in a boat made of reeds. Hell, we might even bump into our son along our way – imagine the look on Marian's face if that were to happen.

And I was smiling myself now, smiling and thinking through all these possibilities when the telephone started ringing. It took me a moment to register that it was our telephone, ringing in our bedroom, and though I lay there and let it ring on, amazingly Marian didn't wake up. She didn't as much as stir. I was tempted to let it carry on ringing, and stay right inside my thoughts, right inside everything that lay ahead for Marian and me, but that other needle inside me kept prodding and so I reached over and picked up the phone.

'Help, please help me', the same familiar voice said. 'Time is running out'.

'What can I do?' I shouted down the receiver. 'Tell me! What can I do?'

THE MEGA-MILLION LOTTERY

I had a distant cousin living in Manhattan's Upper East Side. He was subletting a tiny studio apartment. A long narrow box was how he described it. He said it was like living inside a coffin.

My cousin was having a bad summer. His best friend had died in Mexico. His cat had died in his arms. At any moment his mother was going to die. She was paralysed and had lost her mind. 'It would be an act of compassion if she were to die', my cousin told me over rice bowls. Then he started into a list of all his debts.

He owed the taxman. He owed his accountant. He owed the vet who had tended to his cat. He owed an ex-girlfriend. He owed a former employer. He really owed the guy he was subletting from. There was more, lots more, but I felt it was no longer necessary to tune in. My cousin had found a way to break open the lid on the frustration of his life. The important thing was for him to get it all out.

Because he could no longer afford to live in New York every Friday he played the Mega-Million Lottery. An old

Iranian ran a corner shop on my cousin's street, and this is where he came to buy his lottery tickets.

The first Friday my cousin tried his luck one of his numbers came up.

'You know what this means', said the old Iranian when my cousin showed up to collect his two dollar windfall.

'No', my cousin said.

'You must buy more tickets'.

And so, with each passing Friday, on his way home from visiting his mother in hospital, my cousin would step into the corner shop in order to try out his luck. Soon, he had a routine he performed as he made his lottery purchase.

'I'll have a ticket for the Mega-Million Lottery', he'd say to the old Iranian. 'The winning ticket, please'.

The shopkeeper chuckled and made the sale. On the countertop a cat purred. Steam drifted out of a rice bowl. My cousin patted the cat, smiled at the old shopkeeper and said, 'When I win the Mega-Million Lottery I am sending you and your cat on a holiday to the destination of your choice'. And the shopkeeper chuckled some more.

Pay-up letters for back taxes started to arrive at my cousin's tiny apartment. Demands from his bank. Hospital fees. He wanted to get out of New York and go back to Tokyo where he had lived happily for several years. He told me this over rice bowls we were sharing in a cheap Japanese place he had discovered.

'Do you know that rice is sacred to the Japanese?' he said to me as he picked at his food. 'If they do not get their daily rice they are lost', he continued. It made me think of the way my own mother used to be with cabbage.

'And when they are done eating they leave two grains of rice in the bowl to indicate they are full'.

He stopped eating then, placed his chopsticks on the little ceramic tile beside his bowl, picked out a single grain of rice and held it up between us.

'Without this they are lost. Think about that', he said and let the grain of rice fall into his bowl again.

Over the summer my cousin's debts climbed steadily. Though she no longer recognized her son, his mother clung on to life. In the corner shop he embellished his Friday routine.

'When you sell me the winning ticket I am sending you, your cat and your wife to the destination of your choice', he told the old Iranian who smiled and picked at his rice bowl.

'When you sell me the winning ticket I am sending you, your cat, your wife and all your children on a round-the-world cruise', he told the smiling shopkeeper who lay down his chopsticks, brought his hands together and bowed for his customer and the kind gesture imparted.

'When you sell me the winning ticket I am sending you, your cat, your wife, all your children and all their children back to the old country', he told the shopkeeper who, at once, dropped his chopsticks, clasped his hands, looked to my cousin in horror and pleaded not to be sent back to the old country as it was getting away from the old country that had prompted his flight to America in the first place.

By the end of the summer the Mega-Million Lottery stood at three hundred and sixty-five million dollars. My cousin's mother was fading fast. His bills were mounting. The merest thought of his mother and all that he owed was enough to take away his appetite. He stopped going to the cheap Japanese place. He stopped cooking in the long narrow box he was subletting. He lost weight. Colour drained from his face. Figuring a way out of New York was starting to obsess him. Finally, he received word that his mother had passed away in her sleep.

The Friday after burying his mother my cousin showed up as usual at the corner shop.

'Don't say a word', the old Iranian said. The old shopkeeper then hobbled out from behind his counter, closed up his shop for the day, dragged a rickety stool over to where my cousin was standing and motioned for him to sit down. Then he stepped back behind his counter and pushed his bowl of rice across the counter.

'My friend', he said, handing over the chopsticks. 'You must eat'.

RUNAWAYS

Vanessa and me are going places. London. Paris. Rio de Janeiro. We don't care as long as we're far away from where we are now.

Every day we meet up at the swamp. One day soon the swamp is going to flood our neighbourhood. Vanessa says she hopes it does. So do I. I hope it devours the entire town.

Our town is slap bang in the middle of the country, miles from anywhere, and built inside a hole made out of bog, weeds, mulch and the soggiest soil you could ever see. If that isn't bad enough we are surrounded by a dirty black drain that spends its time fooling everyone into thinking it's a river. There are two sides to our town. The rich side on the hill beyond the railway tracks and the side we live on.

Vanessa is nine and I'm eight. Vanessa's Ma ran away with Chancer Fay a year ago and I've never met my Da. Some day Vanessa is going to be a celebrity. When that happens, no matter where we are, I'm going to be by her side, minding her. We agreed on this ages ago, when we first became friends.

'Where are we off to today?' she asks me when we meet up at the swamp.

'I'm thinking ancient Greece'.

'Never been there', Vanessa says and inside I smile. It's great to find a place Vanessa's never been to.

Once we know where we're going we sit on our rock and look at the Mad Lady. Every day the Mad Lady turns up at the swamp. She stands in the same spot and stares out over the cracked edges, into the muddy reeds. The long silver streaks of her hair look blue in the early sun. The skin on her face looks stretched. 'She's like a stick in the mud', Vanessa says about her. Others say she's crazier than the birds.

From time to time she holds herself and sways. Forward and back. Forward and back. Like a timid wave. Or a change of heart. Neighbours taking the back way up to Steele's Shop give her funny looks. Little Terry Farrell pelts her with balls of muck. When light fades she allows Old Tom Sullivan guide her back inside her house. 'The town is sinking', we hear her say. She has a raspy voice.

'Is your Da still crying?' I ask Vanessa when I feel like talking again.

'He is', she says and rubs the side of her head. Then she slides off our rock and gets ready to leave. She always leaves before I do.

'Same time tomorrow?'

'Of course'.

I stay where I am, watching the swamp. Drifts of steam float above it. Nettles bunch around the cracked edges. Giant dock leaves spread out and billow. There are gnats and clammy webs. Flies dizzy with excitement. Long reedy grasses point to the neverending sky. Ladybirds crawl all over the place. It's a great place to meet up when we don't want to be found. The perfect place.

'Hey', Vanessa calls back to me. 'Do you think I am growing knockers?'

'No way', I answer, without turning around.

Vanessa's Da has been crying for a year. He does it resting his elbows on the kitchen table and holding his face in clenched fists. After a while he slams his fists onto the table and starts shouting at the top of his voice. When Vanessa tiptoes close to him to see if he's alright he swings for her. He does this because he's taking everything out on her. This is what Vanessa says. Luckily for Vanessa his aim needs to improve.

At about a quarter past nine on the last Thursday of every month Phelim Dempsey shows up at our door. He's the star salesman for the feed mill at the edge of town and he gets to drive all over the province offering farmers bags of bull nuts at knockdown prices. Ma says he wouldn't sell bread in a famine, but as soon as he appears she's all smiles and plates of food and cups and saucers. You would think we had royalty wiping its feet on our step.

'Howya Jacinta', Phelim says to Ma as he puts his large grouty hands on as much of her backside as he can. Then he pulls her close. Over her shoulder he winks at me.

As soon as Phelim has eaten what is put down in front of him, the pair of them disappear upstairs. I sit on the stairs, and count seventeen oohs, forty-three aahs and one almighty spasm. About an hour later, when she temporarily reappears, Ma is in great form. 'Here's a euro', she says. 'Now off you go'.

'I should send my Da over to your house', Vanessa says when I tell her all about it.

'Why?'

'All he does is sit with his face in his fists. He needs to see your Ma'.

'I saw him crying in the back lane yesterday'.

'Yeah. Him and my Ma used to go for walks together in the back lane. He can't figure out why she wants to hang around with Chancer Fay'.

'We hang around together because we are going places'.

'That's right. Where to next, partner?'

'I'm thinking South America'.

'Brilliant. Anybody who's anybody has spent time in South America'.

I'm so thrilled I tell her everything I know about South America. I mention the train that reaches through clouds. The desert where it hasn't rained for four hundred years. The lost cities in the jungle mountains. Vanessa hangs on every word I say. It's our best journey yet.

'Are you sure I'm not growing knockers?' she asks me when I'm finished, shoving out her chest. I tell her not to be silly.

I always stay on after Vanessa leaves. I like watching the sun burn mist off the swamp water. The reed grass play with the light. The ladybirds move along dock leaves. Sometimes council men wade around the edges of the swamp. They don't like us being so close. The swamp will swallow you they try to tell us. But we don't care. At the click of a finger, we can be thousands of miles away.

When I spied on them, Ma was sitting on Phelim's lap. He was bucking her up and down and her knockers were heading in many different directions. It was as though they had a mind of their own. I heard fast breathing sounds, little cries, gasps. 'You're an awful woman, Jacinta', I heard him say just before he left. I've never looked at them since.

'I really think my Da should call around to see your Ma', Vanessa says when I give her my report. She isn't asking for travel plans like she usually does. She keeps shoving out her chest and looking at it. She has a scratch under her eye.

'Is he still crying?'

'He's crying and banging his fists on the table and howling like a crazy dog. Then he comes looking for me. His aim is improving'.

'We have no time to lose', I tell her. 'What about some place in Africa?'

'We could look for the source of the Nile'.

'Watch elephants slink into the bush'.

'Chase leopards'.

'I know. We could hang out with baboons'.

We sit quietly together then, making the most of our African adventure.

'Hey, are you sure my knockers aren't growing?' she asks after a few minutes. I roll my eyes and she leaves.

The council men cannot believe there is so much sun. They gather by the edge of the swamp to watch it dry up. But the swamp doesn't dry up. It continues to rise and the council men scratch their heads and try to work out why. They wear long Wellingtons like fishermen and wade through parts of the swamp and test how deep it gets and make notes in little books and they put up warning signs beside the hidden pools. 'Let's go and enjoy the good weather', they then say to each other. 'This is thirsty work'. And they leave again.

When I sit among the reed grass I see the Mad Lady staring into the swamp. I watch jumbo jets ski across the atmosphere. I make friends with two ladybirds. It will be exciting minding Vanessa when she becomes a celebrity. Sometimes I want her beside me at night. I wish she would stop asking me about her knockers.

Ma is singing in the bath when I get home. She sounds like someone who has just fallen off a cliff. Somehow she hears me raiding the presses and calls me into the bathroom.

'Hello, you. Been anywhere interesting today?' she asks, soaping her arms.

'Nowhere special. Are you getting ready for Phelim?'

'Pass me my gown', she says, stepping out of the bath. Luckily she is covered in suds.

'Vanessa's Da wants to come over to see you', I tell her, flinging the gown.

'Does he now?' she says, tying her belt.

'He's been crying for a year. He's going to knock Vanessa into the middle of next month if he doesn't get to see you'.

'Is he indeed?' she says, flicking wet hair away from her face.

'Well, do you have an answer? Phelim won't be here for another couple of days. He could come tomorrow, after dinner say'.

'Here's what you can tell your little pip. Tell her I said she should stick to the children's games she's good at, and leave the other stuff to adults'.

In the morning Vanessa is sitting by the swamp. It's the first time she's arrived before me. I'm praying she doesn't start on about her crying Da and his clenched fists. I have some great places for us to visit today.

'Hey, guess what? I think my knockers have started growing. Look, tell me what you think'.

She's standing up and shoving out her chest again, swaying from side to side in the golden light. She looks exactly as she always does. Her swaying is starting to annoy me.

'I think you're right', I tell her.

'I knew it', she says, beaming now in the sunlight and shoving out her chest even further. 'So, did you ask your Ma?'

'Ask her what?'

'You know, about Da going to see her'.

'Oh yeah, I did ask her'.

'Well, what did she say?'

'She said that you were little more than a pip and to leave grown-ups alone'.

She sits back down at the edge of the swamp. She turns away from me so that she's looking out into the muddy reeds. Then she brings her hands to her face and starts crying. For a moment I don't know what to do. I'm a little afraid. I sit down beside her and listen to her sobby sounds. Then I notice the marks on her neck.

'So where are we off to today?'

She doesn't answer. On a dock leaf two ladybirds are dancing with each other. From a distance I can hear the Mad Lady's raspy voice.

'It's just a silly game', she blurts out through her sobbing, and she stands up and glares down at me.

'We can go to see the Pyramids', I tell her. 'The Mississippi Delta. Or Mexico. We can look for the early burial grounds'.

'You silly little boy', she yells and starts pulling at her hair. She stands up close to me and glares into my face. Her eyes are watery, she has balled her hands and I know we won't be taking any more trips together. We step away from each other and go in opposite directions. Vanessa, home to watch her Da hold his face in his fists until he feels like taking everything out on her. Me, back to listen to my Ma singing in the bath until a quarter past nine on the last Thursday of the month.

HAPPY HOUR

I was in my second-favourite bar, waiting for Happy Hour.
The other place I liked had temporarily shut its doors
because the barman there had put the barrel of the shotgun
he owned in his mouth and was threatening to blow his
head off. Murtagh said he'd been depressed. Reehill said
he was inconsiderate. I said: at what time does the other
place open?

A woman we liked served behind the bar of the second
place. We liked pretty much everything about her. Her
hair. Her eyes. Her skin and teeth. The way she sounded
when she asked us what we would like. The way she could
hang on to complicated orders fired at her from all corners.
The way she became very angry and still retained some
affection for us. Her name was Sharon and she was also a
dancer.

It was an old bar, dimly lit, a place where weary souls
could mingle, rest tired elbows. I liked it best when I was
perched on a high stool in the moments before Happy
Hour began, staring into Sharon's face.

'Are you going to order any time soon?' she asked me when she noticed my puppy-dog look.

'I'm waiting for Happy Hour', I said.

'Aren't we all', she said and moved on to a better prospect.

The great thing about Happy Hour was that it didn't last one hour. It lasted two hours, and every drink on the menu was eligible. Beer. Wine. Paint stripper. It didn't matter what you ordered, your second drink was on the house. Not everybody knew this. Murtagh didn't know. Reehill said he didn't know either, and later he would rile me for not letting him know. Some of those who preferred the first place had no idea Happy Hour even existed. It was hush-hush talk that belonged to this side of town, a piece of information reluctantly released. As soon as word spread about the gun-toting barman, however, some of the thirsty others began to make their way across the river.

My drinking friend, Scully, showed up. We often saw each other at Happy Hour. Sometimes we had amazing conversations and could never remember a thing we said. Sometimes we sat beside each other for six hours without saying a word. Sometimes Scully had money and I didn't, or I had money and Scully didn't. He was seven years younger than me, a little brother I never had, and ours was a fellowship based on a fondness for early booze. We made the most of what we had.

'Hey, Clem. Did you hear what's happening across the river?' he asked as soon as he was comfortable on the stool next to me.

'Yes'.

'Can you believe it? I didn't even know he owned a shotgun. If I did I would have asked him for a loan of it. You know what this means, don't you?'

'No'.

'It means we'll have every lowlife from across the river showing up in here this afternoon'.

'What are we, Scully?' I asked my friend.

'What are we? Oh, you're funny, Clem. Hey, has Happy Hour started yet?'

'No'.

'I'll wait so'.

I looked at my friend. His left eye was bloodshot. His nose was a bulbous mess, his teeth were turning brown. Hardly into his forties and already way past his use-by date. A skin-and-bone ruin, a sketch of a man. Once upon a time he had been a student of medicine. So the story went. Eating cranberries stalls the aging process he told me one night. Make sure you have crescent moons in your fingernails. I didn't know why he told me these things.

'Hey, Clem, did I tell you I was thinking of going back to work for two months? Then I might go somewhere'.

'Where will you go, Scully?'

'I haven't decided yet. But I will think about it. You should think about the future, Clem. It's coming, you know. Look, there's a woman over there. I'll be back in a few minutes'.

I had lost my latest job after trying to set a man alight by dousing him with a jerry-can of petrol and then flicking a lit match. The man was my boss. He had refused me a pay rise, told me I needed to use my initiative more often. Later, I had walked unannounced into his office and let him have all the initiative I could summon. By the time they got to him he was a charred mess. That's a joke. His sleeves were barely singed. And aside from never wanting to see me again my boss had no interest in taking the matter any further. After that, word got around and I was through working for a while. It was a small town.

'Hey, Clem, is it Happy Hour yet?' Scully called out to me from a low stool by the back wall.

'You just asked me that', I replied.

'Well is it or isn't it?' I heard a second voice screech. It was the woman Scully had joined. She had black reedy hair, a wrinkled powder-white face, a long emaciated throat Scully was doing his best to nibble. I looked from one to the other and wondered what their child would look like.

Time nudged a little closer to Happy Hour and Scully was right. The place was filling up with the cream of the town's lowlife, wasters, dropouts and all-round misfits. Stab Nolan, Horse Kelly and Boomerang McCaffrey walked in. For the past twenty years Boomerang had been saying he was leaving, getting out of town, never to return. There was a rumour he had once made it as far as the motorway, but had turned around again upon spotting someone he had been successfully avoiding. Teabag Maguire walked in, along with his sidekick, Frosty Mitchell. Frosty was half-barred which meant he could come in but only drink tea. Teabag wouldn't pay for his tea. He asked for cups of hot water and did the rest himself, courtesy of the pouch of tealeaves he had been walking the streets with for the past twenty or thirty years. Jimmy Slice walked in. His wife had run away with a mystery man Jimmy swore he was going to hack into little pieces and then eat. I hadn't seen some of this lot smile in over a quarter of a century. They were tough and resilient and I knew there was a part of themselves they hadn't given birth to yet, some vital quality they were saving for when it really mattered. I couldn't help but envy them.

'Hey, Clem'.

'Hey, Teabag. Hey, Frosty'.

'Hey, Clem'.

'Hey, Jimmy. Hey, Boomerang. What's the story yonder?'

'Ah, he's still got the gun cocked. They're not letting anyone near the place'.

They made their way along the bar, claimed a place and waited their turn to be served. As soon as he spotted them Scully was up out of his chair and quickly forgetting about the neck he was nibbling.

'Hey, you lot! We don't want you in here, polluting this side of town. Go and drink somewhere else. Tell them, Sharon'.

'Tell them what?'

'To flake off'.

Sharon rolled her eyes and placed a cup of tea and a cup of hot water in front of Frosty and Teabag. Kelly and Nolan turned around to face Scully.

'Hey, Scully', Nolan said, nudging his friend, 'are you still pissing off rooftops?'

'I heard it was the double decker bus he pisses off'.

'I'll piss on you, Kelly, if you don't –'

'Alright, Scully', Sharon butted in and Scully put on his best I-am-the-victim face. Then he pointed at me.

'Clem knows what I'm talking about. Tell her, Clem. Tell her before this lot start taking over'.

'Scully!' Sharon tried again, with a little more vehemence and, reluctantly, Scully sat back down beside his new lady friend.

Sharon was soon busy at the beer taps. I looked over her shoulder, caught my reflection in the mirror by the optics. I looked like I had been dragged across a lengthy gravel trench. Pitted eyes. Warped nose. Bald patches in my stubble. Fifty years of age and I was trying to set my fellow man on fire. In truth, all I could see were ghosts. They drifted through the dim light, mingled with some punters they had taken a liking to, then passed through the flaking walls, back inside whatever netherworld they occupied. I envied them too.

I glanced at my wrist. Then I remembered that I had lost my watch at the card table in the back room. A pair of eights taking on a king-high flush. 'Trump that', I murmured at the floating ghosts. As soon as I did Scully was back beside me.

'I told you, didn't I?'

'What did you tell me, Scully?'

'They're only here because their usual place is off-limits'.

'Relax, Scully. It's almost Happy Hour'.

'Hey, Clem, remind me what happens'.

'You buy a drink and you get two drinks'.

'What happens if I buy two drinks?'

'Then you get four'.

'You mean to tell me if I buy four drinks I'll get six?'

'No. You'll get eight'.

'Eight!'

'That's right'.

'I like the sound of that. Hey, Clem, I think we should keep it between ourselves. Now excuse me, I have to take this good news back to Cloda'.

I watched him shuffle awkwardly through the bar. It was a nervy, staccato movement, every step fraught with suspicion. At any moment it seemed his legs would collapse under him. Making sure they couldn't see him, he stuck out a dirty tongue at Nolan and Kelly. When I swung around in my stool again Sharon was smiling at me, the fingers of one hand poised on a beer tap, the other holding up an empty glass.

'That smile deserves an award', I said.

'You ready yet?'

'A minute or two more'.

'Tell me something. If Happy Hour was abolished would I ever see you again?'

'You could come with me'.

'First, I'd like to know what you are made from'.

'You and me both', I said, though, of course, I no longer cared. Way back, at an early stage, I wish I could've known. A bundle of fret and fear? A dollop of unconcern? Tiny drops of malice? I could've flushed it all away and ordered a new design. These days I couldn't watch someone eat a plate of food or occupy themselves poetically in the weak light without wanting to replicate the experience for myself.

'Penny for them', I heard Sharon say, she was still in front of me. For her I could have made up a happy-ending story for free.

Patch Fahy walked in. And Gloom Grehan. And Pillbox Roche. For the past twenty years Pillbox had been telling anyone who would listen that he was dying of an incurable disease. Rabies. Flesh-eating bacteria. An irreversible case of the runs. It didn't matter. 'I'm a goner', was all he'd say if anyone tried to get him to be more specific. When he was ignored he took his woes out on female American tourists. Freewheeling Frank walked in. Once upon a time Frank had mowed down a student with his motorbike. He hadn't shaved or cut his hair since. Nobody I knew had any idea what he looked like. He claimed to have once drank eleven pints of lager before needing the toilet.

'Hey, Clem'.

'Hey, Patch. Hey, Gloom'.

'Hey, Clem'.

'Hey, Pillbox. Hey, Frank. How's the stand-off going?'

'Ah, hard to know. Every so often he takes the gun out and starts going on about some woman called Deborah. Then he gets fed up talking and shoves the gun back in again. Hard to know how it will pan out'.

Sharon filled more drinks. Glasses clinked the time of day, heartsick man, the end of everything. Scully was out of his chair again.

'What are you lot doing in here?'

'Don't be like that, Scully. We're not staying in this dump all evening'.

'Hey, Sharon, did you hear that? He called this place a dump'.

'Relax, Scully, it's almost Happy Hour'.

'Grehan, don't tell me to relax if you don't want to get knocked down'.

'Scully! Stop annoying my customers'.

'They're not your customers, Sharon. They belong –'

'Scully! You're on a yellow card'.

Scully froze where he stood, his arms spread out in supplication, his mouth wide open. He looked around to make sure everyone could see that he was the one singled out by Sharon. Nobody paid any attention to him. He made his way over to me.

'Clem! Did you hear what she said? Yellow card!'

'That's funny, Scully'.

'We have a good mind not to stay here. We should boycott'.

'I'm not missing Happy Hour', I told my friend and he shuffled off again.

I tried to imagine the place emptied of all these faces. Every one of them vanished somewhere else with their lives, to some sort of beer heaven perhaps, or hell. Already I knew I would quickly forget them, the thought was enough to send me into a tailspin.

Sharon was in front of me again.

'Are you ready for a drink?'

'Is it time?'

'Let's not fall out over a slow clock'.

'Don't spoil it, Sharon. These are my favourite minutes'.

She smiled and shook her head and as she leaned away from me I closed my eyes and absorbed as much of her as I could. Vanilla. Almond. Something else. When I opened my eyes again she was standing at one end of the bar, taking it all in. 'So many fallen angels', I could have sworn I heard her whisper.

Around me the talk was of the fatalistic barman across the river.

'Why does he have to do it in a pub?'

'I know of a teacher who hanged herself in a classroom'.

'He should throw himself in front of the Dublin train'.

'Or down Maher's Well'.

'Sleeping pills. It's the only way'.

'Not a lot of theatre in that'.

'Pain-free, though'.

'Well, if he is going to do it I wish to hell he'd hurry up. I'm not staying here all night dinking tea'.

'Relax, Frosty, it's almost Happy Hour'.

'What am I going to do with you lot?' Sharon said with her hands on her hips and a few of them got busy letting her know.

Scully was back on the stool beside me. I remembered I had given him a tenner. I thought Happy Hour might be a good time to tease him, so I asked him for it.

'I gave it to you last Friday', he said.

'I was at home last Friday, Scully'.

'Don't be silly, Clem. You're never at home'.

'At what time did you give it back to me?'

'At what time? Happy Hour. That's at what time'.

'Scully, why did you sit beside me?'

'It's about that tenner. I was wondering could I borrow it again. Ah, would you look at that. First they come in here to drink our beer. Then they try to steal our women'.

I turned in my stool and followed Scully's gaze. Nolan and Kelly were sitting in low chairs, laughing at something

Scully's woman was saying. Briefly, the three of them looked over at us. Scully was on his way.

And came to me thoughts of a girl I fell in love with when I was fourteen. A mouse with a smile that projected both affection and disdain. I spent an entire summer following her. Around the town on Saturday. Down to the courts when she took up tennis. Through the estates I skipped when word reached me she was on the move. My heart akimbo. Later someone pointed out a sister and I fell for her too. A cousin appeared and I wanted to cut myself into three pieces. I should have done it too. Would have saved me a lot of foolishness.

Behind me I heard a woman's scream, then a glass shattering. I looked around and saw Scully holding his hands up to his face, lines of blood already appearing through his fingers. Nolan and Kelly spun him around and pushed him towards the toilets. The woman hissed after him, clawed the longest fingernails I had ever seen, turned away and quickly left.

'That lad!' Sharon said, shaking her head. She grabbed a towel and followed him into the toilets. A minute later I heard her scream my friend's name. Then she was frogmarching him through the bar as the blood dripped from his hand-held face onto the floor.

'Will you not let him stay, Sharon?' I called after her.

'I have a day off next year. He can come back then'.

'That's not fair, Sharon', Scully said over his shoulder. 'Frank went into the ladies and pissed in the potpourri. You let him stay'.

'Frank? Is that true?'

'Ah, Sharon. No one in here ever uses the ladies'.

'I DO!'

'She has you there, Frank'.

'Out Scully!' Sharon roared.

Scully stood with his back to the bar door. There was a bleeding gash beneath his right eye, but he seemed more interested in his blood-smeared fingers. He brought his hands up to his face, then raised them high over his head like a priest giving thanks. He shrugged briefly, and pushed his way through the door. Sharon watched him all the way.

'It's that time', she said to me when she was back behind the counter.

'Give me a bottle, Sharon', I said. 'The biggest you have'.

'You know what your problem is', she said, passing me the vodka. 'You don't know how to play the trump cards you have'.

'I like you, Sharon', I said. 'When the time comes I want you in my lifeboat'.

'Happy Happy Hour, Clem'.

I paid for the bottle and walked out of there.

Later, Scully and me were stumbling around the old harbour, taking turns with the vodka. I watched the swans, the old lady toss her crumbs, the madman patrolling the open quay with his invisible rifle. As soon as he spotted Scully and me he knew something wasn't right. He raised his weapon, took aim and put two caps inside each of us. Instinctively, Scully grasped his chest and jerked backwards and, as he fell, I saw the sun bleed into the horizon.

And I remember making my way onto the upper deck of a slow moving bus. It had an open top and I welcomed the sea breeze with open arms, clutched the soft swirls to me, kissed the salty tang. Then I heard someone calling my name.

It was Scully. Of course it was. He was on the bus too.

'Hey, Scully, your zipper is undone'.

'I know. Look, there's a woman. I'll be back in a few minutes'.

He stood up unsteadily and wobbled across the aisle. I looked out over the open deck. Evening light, falling angels, the world spinning beneath me. Scully was speaking again, offering his resilient words.

'Hey, lady, tell me something. Have you ever been shot at?'

The woman scooted in as far as she could go and looked the other way. Scully tugged his shirt out of his trousers, ripped it open and sank to his knees. 'Look at me', he pleaded, dribbling tusks of saliva onto his bared flesh. A moment later the bus jerked to a standstill and a young man holding a microphone appeared.

'You can't be up here', he screamed at Scully. 'This is a tour bus'.

'Leave him be', I slurred. 'Can't you see he is mortally wounded?'

THAI FOOD

I was passing through the town I had grown up in and had arranged to meet my father. I hadn't seen him in six years. In that time I had worked as a greeting card salesman, a data entry clerk, a night watchman at an amusement arcade, and a stock man for a fertiliser company that went bust. At various times I had also been away, seeing parts of the world. I was at a stage in my life when drifting aimlessly from year to year still seemed to be a good idea.

'Well look who it is. It's been a while, son', he said to me as soon as he opened the door of his house and clapped a hand on my shoulder.

'How are you?' I said, putting an arm awkwardly around him. He returned the gesture long enough for me to get the combined whiff of aftershave and whiskey.

'Never better', he said, letting go of me. 'Listen, are you hungry? I am. Let's go and get some Thai food. A Thai restaurant finally opened a couple of months ago. It's really great. The food isn't bad either'.

By the time he had finished his greeting he had already pulled the door after him, and was stepping quickly towards his car. Dutifully, I followed and sat into the passenger seat alongside him.

'You're going to love this place', he said, as we drove the short drive into town. 'Cyril Farrell recommended it to me shortly after it opened and I haven't missed a week since. I can't believe it took so long for one to open. Every other town has one'.

I wasn't too concerned about the restaurant, the long wait for it, whether I would like the food or not. My father seemed happy to blather on about it, however, and I was glad I had made the effort to visit him.

He parked his car on the street, more or less outside the restaurant. It was early evening, much of the town had emptied out. It was very quiet to tell the truth.

'I think we're still on time for the early bird', he said, moving briskly towards the restaurant. 'You're in for a treat', he said, holding the restaurant door for me.

Once seated, I realised how quiet it really was. The place had that soulless atmosphere that infects establishments seldom frequented. There were far too many tables and place settings, even for a weekend night which it was not. It was a Tuesday evening, and my father and I were the only customers. After a moment or two a man appeared through the double swing doors separating the restaurant from the kitchen area. He was a trim-looking man, short, a little into his fifties I would have guessed, and dressed in an immaculately pressed navy suit. The owner, I assumed.

'Ah, good evening, Frank', he said to my father. 'And what can I do for you today?'

'Two early bird specials and two beers, Ken', said my father. 'Oh, by the way, this is my son. He's a real high flyer. Son, meet Ken, owner of this fine establishment'.

'A pleasure to meet you', Ken said, nodding in my direction.

'He's just back from an all-over-the-world trip. He's been everywhere. I'd say he's even been to your neck of the woods. A high flyer. Any sign of those beers yet?'

Ken raised his left hand and as he started to retreat I noticed he was missing his thumb and little finger. As soon as he was out of sight my father leaned across the table to me, as though preparing to impart a long-held secret. 'His name isn't Ken', he said to me in a low voice. 'But I'm not able to pronounce his real name'. And he sat back into his chair again.

I didn't know what to say to him. We hadn't spoken to each other in any meaningful way in a long time. He and my mother had divorced almost five years ago. She had moved to the coast and put her life back together. My father had carried on as though nothing had happened.

I thought that maybe I could begin with some fun stuff. Stuff that might get a laugh. There was plenty from my travels I could share with him. The time a young Cuban couple had gypped me into shelling out an outrageous price for six Mojitos and one hundred fake cigars. The time I had to bribe a Peruvian policeman in order to avoid spending a night in the clink. Maybe I could tell him about the time I was mistaken for a bear while hiking in Canada. I went over some of these stories in my head, but they didn't seem to be worth repeating. They had lost their lustre. Plus, I didn't remember the experiences as being all that much fun at the time. What, I asked myself, was going to make any of it fun in this soulless setting?

As I was mulling this over Ken reappeared with a pair of uncapped beers which he set down on the table. At once, my father took one, brought it quickly to his mouth and drained about half of it before setting it down again. Ken hovered by our table, looking from his watch to my father.

'You want an omelette, Frank?'

'No, Ken. Just the early bird special. Two of them'.

'You want an omelette, son?' he said again, this time looking at me.

'Ken', my father said, getting ready to finish off his beer. 'Two early bird specials. With steamed rice. No omelettes, OK. And bring two more beers'.

Ken accepted my father's answer, but he sulked a little, looked at his watch again and shook his head as he retreated back behind the swing doors. I decided to skip the funny stories.

'So. How is your mother?' my father asked.

'She's well', I answered, relieved to have something to say. 'It was her idea I come to see you. She says hello, hopes you are well'.

'Oh really', he said, gulping down some beer. 'Tell me something, did she ever figure out how to cook a stew? No wait, I think I know the answer to that one'.

'Much of her cooking still leaves a lot to be desired', I conceded.

'Do you remember the time she served us turnips every day for a week? Jesus! Did you know she stopped letting me visit? For a while there she even refused to answer the phone. Didn't stop her taking my money, though. A leopard doesn't change its spots, eh, son. Did you come across any leopards on your big adventure?'

'Not really'.

'A good job. They scratch, you know'.

I said nothing, instead took one of the beers in front of me and swallowed most of it.

'I think she still mentions me at mealtime. Usually she has just positioned her hands into a stranglehold. Or is considering further uses for her carving knife!' He said all this, laughed and gulped the remains of the second beer.

Our early bird specials arrived. Again Ken stood over our table, waiting, I presumed, for us to taste the food. My father raised one of the empty beer bottles and shook it.

Ken took it and returned with two more. This time he didn't wait about. From inside the double doors issued a loud clanging sound followed by a wolf-like howl. Ken excused himself and returned rapidly into the kitchen.

'And how is your sister?' my father asked me, drinking from one of the new arrivals.

'Oh, you know'.

'Does she still want the whole world to go away?' he said, chuckling some more, and he paused with his fork in mid-air, and smiled, as though silently reflecting upon the borne-out truth of some conclusion he had come to a long time ago.

'Are they still living together?'

'Yes', I said.

'Jesus! They make some pair. I suppose they belong together – like crutches. Know what I mean?'

He stopped talking and stared down at his of plate of food. Raised voices from the kitchen reached us. Tumbling pots. A high-pitched screech. He didn't seem to notice.

'This sauce isn't as good as it usually is', he said after his pause. 'It's a little thin. Don't you think it's a little thin?'

I hadn't really noticed the sauce. Actually, I had hardly begun my meal. Merely mixed in some of the steamed rice with the meat and vegetables.

In any event, I didn't have time to give an answer to the question. The double doors spun open and Ken dashed into the restaurant. He was closely pursued by a man of his own age and stature – the restaurant's chef. He was brandishing a gleaming cleaver and he was seething. Ken ran among the tables, jumped a couple of chairs before turning to his pursuer as though considering a face-off. But sight of the cleaver hastened his flight once more and, displaying agility and athleticism uncommon in a man of his age, he established a wiry movement that enabled him to elude his pursuer's continually flaying arms. My father glanced at the unfolding commotion, took a long drink and chuckled to himself. Then he pointed his fork at me.

'So. What have you been up to?'

'Oh, you know. This and that'.

'Sounds great. You must have thought I had died and been buried'.

'Huh?'

'How is your rice? I think myself the rice could have been fluffier'.

I didn't have a thing to say about the rice. Besides, it was difficult to comment, what with all that family stuff suddenly swimming around inside me and now a cleaver-wielding chef intent on causing grievous bodily harm.

It looked as though Chef's persistence was about to pay off. He had cornered Ken at the angle of two of the restaurant walls, and was gently prodding Ken backwards with the cleaver. Sensing his moment had finally arrived, Chef moved closer and closer to his prey, bristling. Then Ken sprang upon his adversary and the two men quickly tumbled to the floor whereupon they started to roll around haphazardly, all the time clinging to each other as though their lives depended on it. I heard my father talking again.

'I had a dream the other night. I was present at my own funeral. I was looking at myself being laid out in the sitting room, looking at Mickey Finlay as he screwed down the lid of the coffin, looking at Tom Ward as he made a proper hayms of lowering the coffin into the grave. Then I woke up'.

'Sounds spooky'.

'That's right. I got your card from that place in Argentina'.

'Patagonia'.

'Yes, Patagonia – that place sounds perfect'.

'I'm planning to go back', I said.

'Hold on a second, will you'.

He got up from the table and walked towards the kitchen doors. He disappeared through a smaller door to the right, and just as quickly reappeared, carrying a beer in either hand. Ken and Chef were still struggling on the floor together. On his way back to our table my father looked at them and nodded approvingly.

'Have you been to Japan?' he said, sitting back down.

'No', I said, 'I haven't been there'.

'Did I tell you I bumped into Emmet Clarke? He had a girl with him, she looked Japanese. She was wheeling a buggy. Anyway, he told me he was living in England now, near Oxford – where he studied. He has a PhD in thermodynamics or astrophysics, something like that, it sounded good. Anyway, he was asking for you and wondering what you were up to. I wish I knew myself I said to him'.

Chef and Ken were back on their feet, facing each other in the main aisle of the restaurant. I almost expected them to bow to each other and respectfully withdraw. Then, via the swing doors, a third person entered the restaurant – a young girl, not long into her teens. I assumed she was the owner's daughter. She had his colouring and posture, and was wearing a judo suit. She approached the two men and without warning she kick-boxed her father to the ground and subsequently straddled her prone victim and proceeded to steadily pummel his chest with her little fists. Chef egged her on. My father raised his beer in her direction and smiled. What had Ken done to this girl to warrant such ferocity, I wondered? What dark secrets did those pounding little fists contain?

Arranging the knife and fork in front me, I looked to my father, and for the first time noticed the purple blotches in his cheeks, the sagging beneath his eyes, how life had finally begun to stretch him.

'Thanks for the meal', I said to him.

'What do you mean?' he replied. 'You've hardly touched your food. Not that I blame you. It's never been as bland as this. I might have to consider going elsewhere'.

'Thanks', I said again and stood out of my chair.

'Where are you going? Hey, come back. I want to talk to you. I have some things I want to say'.

I paused at the door of the restaurant. I looked back at my father and then at the unfolding scene on the restaurant floor. The girl's arms were pummelling away for all they were worth. Chef was standing to one side, the cleaver resting in the fold of his crossed arms. Taking in this unlikely scene a million different things I could've said to my father down through the years raced through my mind. But I knew it was too late now, that the passage of time had turned over something inside both of us, and sent us in opposing directions – not unlike the behaviour towards each other of magnets that can never touch. And if there had been a time when we could have sat across a table from each other and entered into the kind of conversation that chimed with the patterns of our lives, it had managed to elude us. And so I pulled open the door and walked out of the restaurant and on down the street of the town I had grown up in and, for a brief and acutely painful moment, I wondered if I would ever see him again.

Elizabeth Taylor and the
Tour de France Cyclist

Sometimes, after they had made love, Audrey spoke to Ciaran of things he felt he didn't understand. It might begin with a playful comment, something relating to their time together, a habit of Ciaran's she had noticed. Soon she would trail off in another direction as though her initial observation was only a prelude to what she really wanted to say. Often she spoke of her life as a mother and as a wife. Of her early dreams.

'When I was your age I was going to be an actress', she told him. 'I watched movies of all my favourite plays. *Hamlet. Macbeth. Cat on a Hot Tin Roof.* I took classes. Joined a theatre group. At rehearsals they said I had it. I was going to play Ophelia. Lady Macbeth. And Maggie the Cat. But come the big night I could never remember my lines. I was so nervous, you see. It was very frustrating'.

She spoke eloquently, Ciaran thought. He liked her choice of words, and also the way she sounded every syllable in the words she chose. He sensed her sadness, and the regret in her voice, but he felt unable to respond. Instead, he slid down in the bed and sought out her thighs.

When he was cycling home, Ciaran thought of Fiona. He thought of her freckled nose and swinging pigtails. Her bold smile and kicking feet. He thought of the dirt lane they would transform into an untamed wilderness. And of the characters they used to put in their made-up adventures: the ragman picking berries in the ditch; Moses, the three-legged dog; the mad woman called Doodle. He thought of postcards Fiona would write to him when her parents whisked her away to some foreign destination. He thought of secrets they shared, joys and pains, ambitions and bitter ends. He thought of Fiona's fearlessness, her easy way around people much older than her, her knack for always saying the right thing. Fiona and Ciaran. Inventors. Explorers. Discoverers of all things. Neighbours. Best friends. Kindred spirits. Five years ago, when Ciaran was twelve, she had been knocked off her bicycle by a truck. She died in the ambulance on its way to the hospital. She had just turned thirteen.

He thought of other things when he was out on his bike. Decisions he would soon have to make. His inability to make lasting friendships. His constant desire to be away from people. His quiet need for approval. Often he caught himself inventing unlikely scenarios that might assist this need. Usually, they involved Ciaran placing himself as the hero at the scene of an emergency. Swimming out to save a drowning woman. A last-ditch dash into a burning building to rescue a distraught mother's trapped child. He saw himself as a doctor successfully performing an outrageous feat of surgery in some impossible-to-reach location. He put these heroic imaginings down to the solitary bicycle trips he took himself on, the easy movement and the freedom he felt while coasting along the quiet country roads he chose for his excursions. Once he had left the city behind, its crowds and noise and unpredictable traffic, Ciaran felt something dissolve inside him, a barrier that was always present and that he could never account for. Once out on his bicycle, coasting through the heather fields and furze bushes lining either side of a favourite back-road, no flight of fancy was too outrageous for his imagination.

Audrey was his mother's book-club friend, lived five miles outside town in a bungalow with a very large garden. Several weeks ago, at the start of summer, Audrey had mentioned to Ciaran's mother that her garden was in an awful state. Her husband didn't care about it and, besides, he was away. Her own son didn't know what a weed looked like and, besides, he was away too. She didn't know where to start. It's a fully grown jungle, she said very theatrically. It was pocket money, Ciaran thought when asked would he do some work on it. Also, it would get him out on his bicycle, out on the country roads he craved. He would be away from people. His latest bicycle trip was his seventh or eight out to his mother's friend's house. So far, he had done little gardening.

On his first visit they had walked around the garden he was supposed to tend. It was wild and unkempt, and Ciaran thought it would take longer than the summer to make it look like something resembling the neighbouring places. She had offered him a glass of wine on his second visit. She poured herself one too. 'Drinking at this hour is *so* decadent', she said, clinking his glass. He drank the wine too quickly, and allowed her top up his glass when she was ready for another herself. His third visit they sat close to each other on her sofa and he could smell her perfume; taste her lipstick, almost, when she leaned into him, took his hand and placed it inside her sweater. The flesh felt soft and he wanted more. His fourth visit she lay back on the sofa and showed him what to do as he moved clumsily on top of her. On his next three visits they made love in her bedroom. She told him not to take everything so quickly, and he was glad of her experience in these matters. With each successive visit, he cycled faster and faster to her bungalow.

Her husband was somewhere in the Middle East, on an engineering project. Something like that, she wasn't sure. It kept him away for months at a time. 'The money is good and the suntan is free', she said to Ciaran. 'Remember the ad', she went on and waited for him to supply the punch-line. Then, she remembered who she was with and pulled him to her.

She liked to dress well, wore makeup, always smelled of perfume. She waved her hands when she spoke. Her son was one year older than Ciaran. He had just finished his first year at college, was studying French and film. Ciaran had never heard of such a combination. 'He's spending his summer in France. His name is Romeo and he is my finest achievement', Audrey said about her son. Ciaran didn't want to hear about Romeo or where he was or what he was studying or the sense of achievement he gave to his mother. 'Is he mad at you for calling him Romeo?' was all Ciaran had to say on the subject. Audrey laughed loudly at that, and for a long time. So Ciaran slid down in the bed and started nibbling the insides of her thighs, precisely where she had shown him.

Sometimes, they lay together in the afternoon and watched a movie of a play she liked. She knew many parts and lying there in the boy's arms she often supplied the dialogue of characters for whom she had a particular fondness. 'I want a big sloppy kiss', she begged of Ciaran as they lay together watching Elizabeth Taylor toy with Richard Burton during the opening sequence of *Whose Afraid of Virginia Woolf*. Though not fully sure what to make of all the theatrics, Ciaran enjoyed her matinee performances, and he reached his arms further around her flesh and held her firmly.

Sometimes, they lay together, saying nothing. It was an easy silence, and Ciaran never felt as though she was waiting for him to speak. One afternoon she asked him what he was going to do with his life. He couldn't think of anything to say to that either. It was a question he didn't like. Teachers at school asked him, his mother and father. He even remembered Fiona asking him, when they cycled together. Back then he didn't know either. Fiona knew, though. She told him he should be a cyclist in the Tour de France. Either that or a vet. He had no idea where that had come from. He just remembered her saying it. What about you, he had asked his best friend. I'm going to Africa, she said. I'm going to mind elephants.

'Penny for them', he heard Audrey say into his thoughts, as she snuggled into him, and he found himself shaking his head. 'So make a wish', she said next. 'And you don't have to tell me what it is'.

Later, when he was cycling back to town, he thought of possible answers to Audrey's request. But nothing he thought of satisfied him, and he allowed his mind wander.

He had taught Fiona how to ride a bicycle. She didn't want to at first, but Ciaran encouraged her, told her how freeing it felt coasting along the back roads, through the summer breeze, amidst the wildness of the coastal countryside. It was the solitude, Ciaran explained. Few cars travelled the back roads. The odd rambler. Seldom another cyclist even. He loved the long summer days. The colours in the evening sky. The smells of heather and phlox, the rhododendrons.

When Fiona got the hang of her bicycle he brought her around the loop he liked to do. It took about forty-five minutes. After an early climb the ground levelled out. In the distance the bay came into view. The golf club. The little bogland lakes.

Fiona pedalled confidently, often coasting past him on downhill stretches before the upward grind kicked in again. She was fearless, Ciaran thought to himself many times. In no time she was enjoying the cycle loop as much as he did – so much so she even started making trips by herself. The day of the accident she had asked him to go with her. She had discovered a new road, quiet and rugged, with great views from the summit of a steep climb. But he hadn't felt like a cycle. He had come off his bike the day before, after allowing Fiona coax him into freewheeling no-hands down another sharp slope. A pothole had appeared just as the road started to flatten out, Ciaran hadn't seen it, and he had gone over the handlebars. Somehow, a bloody elbow was all he had come away with, but it was enough to keep him off his bike for a day or two.

In time to come he knew he had lost something precious. He sensed it when he was around others, in the school yard, at home with his parents, with other relatives and neighbourhood people Fiona had always amused with her unusual assertions. He sensed it when he considered some of her ambitions. I intend to bike it to India she would tell him along their cycles together. Then I'll take a snowmobile across Siberia. In four summers time I am going to walk to the tip of South America. Most of all he sensed this loss when he was by himself, cycling. And there – it came to him, something he could wish for. To go back to that fateful day, to take up Fiona's cycling invitation. And, maybe, things would turn out differently.

When he arrived home and put his bike in the garden shed and drew back the patio door and stepped into the kitchen, his mother was sitting at the table with a glass of red wine.

'It's late', she said.

'I know. I was clearing some awkward bushes'.

'I was calling your mobile. I was worried'.

'There's no coverage out there. I had it switched off'.

'How is the garden?'

'It's a battle, but I think I'm winning', he replied, then pleaded exhaustion and made his way upstairs to his room.

More of the summer passed. July downpours and with them the various events that marked this time of year – Film Week, the Arts Festival, the big race meet which brought more people into town, thousands of them, and galloped the summer into August. Ciaran stayed longer and longer at Audrey's house. He told his mother the garden needed lots of work. Occasionally, he even grabbed a spade and uprooted some weeds. Cleared away nastier looking bramble. Mowed a section of lawn. Audrey applauded his efforts and carried into the garden a tray of wine and crackers. She spread a blanket upon which they lay and feasted and fondled until the sun started to go down. Ciaran arrived home later and later.

One such afternoon her telephone rang. Audrey stepped inside the house, closing the door after her. From where he was lying, Ciaran could hear her laugh, talk a little. Then she was back on the blanket beside him, loosening her clothes, asking him to touch her, telling him what to do, guiding his eager hands.

'Was that your husband?' he asked afterwards.

'No. It was Romeo. He misses his mommy. He's such a sweet boy'.

Later that same day Audrey dressed up for her lover. She wanted to perform one of her favourite Elizabeth Taylor scenes for him, and she went through her wardrobe in search of a suitable costume. She found a wig and a gown with a corset which Ciaran tied as tightly as he could. She reddened her cheeks, thickened her eyelashes with some sort of paste, darkened her eyes with liner.

Then Ciaran took his place on the sofa and watched her present herself, and sashay across the room as she delivered her lines. Eventually he reached out his arms and hauled her onto the sofa beside him and began unfastening clips and undoing strings while seeking out her thighs with his lips.

'You better stop', Audrey said, dragging Ciaran up beside her. 'It's getting dark'.

'I'm not going home', he said. 'I want to stay here all night. I want to spend the night licking every part of you'.

It was practically black when he set off on his bicycle. His bike had no lights, and he didn't have a reflective armband. About two miles from town he rounded a sharp corner a little too quickly, and drifted across the road just as an oncoming car was facing into the same turn. The driver saw him and swerved, and braked to a stop. But Ciaran didn't stop. He kept going, pedalling faster and faster, until the corner was well behind him, and the lights of the city had started to appear. He wasn't in the least bit fazed by his near miss. If anything the experience added to the euphoria coursing through him after his time with Audrey. Not since before Fiona had died had he felt so at ease with himself, so comfortable inside his own skin. Watching the city lights emerge in the darkness, it occurred to him that he didn't want anything beyond what he now had. Decisions were no longer necessary. He didn't need to make wishes.

When he arrived home his mother was in the kitchen with her glass of wine.

'Please tell me you didn't cycle home without any lights'.

'It was OK. It's a quiet road'.

'You know I don't like you cycling in the dark'.

'Sorry'.

'So, how is the garden?'

'I think I'm getting there'.

'You certainly put in long hours. Is it not hard work, all that raking?'

'Oh, you know. I hardly notice. The hours go by so fast out there'.

'So Audrey says'.

'Oh, you were talking to her'.

'Yes. I called to see what was keeping you. She said you'd just left. And I wanted to arrange calling out to see her'.

'Oh'.

'Yes, I might go out some day with you. Inspect your handiwork. We could take the car. Or we could cycle together. That might be fun. What happened your neck?'

'Sorry?'

'You have a bruise on your neck. What happened?'

His hand drifted to the arch of his neck, to one of the places Audrey's busy mouth had found earlier. Blood throbbed inside him at the thought of her. 'Oh', he gasped, trying to suppress what he was feeling. 'A bit of bramble nicked me'.

August progressed and the weather settled, and with it Audrey took her costumes out into the garden where Ciaran lay down on the blanket and watched her soft feet move across the grass, listening and not listening to her words as she slowly peeled a glove from an arm, tossed her wig into his lap, and, at the boy's enthusiastic bidding, tantalizingly removed other unnecessary garments. He didn't dare mention his mother to Audrey. And she smiled at him, as though privy to what was going through his ever-lusty mind.

At his mother's insistence he bought a reflective armband, and a fluorescent vest, and front and back lights for his bike, which, in nights to come, flashed on and off in the darkness as he sped euphorically towards town having spent the previous hours pulling Audrey out of various costumes amidst wild flowers and thorny bushes.

One late August evening he asked her to dress only in underwear, and watched as she powdered her face, laced up her bodice, rolled dark stockings up her legs, fastened suspender clips. He asked her to put on a wig, one she hadn't used before. Her wigs transformed her. It was like he was in the presence of a different person. He felt distanced from her during these performances, and this unfamiliarity kindled further desire. He had already wrestled her laughingly to the ground when the telephone starting ringing.

'Stop', she said, dragging herself away from his groping. 'I need to take this call'.

He sat up and watched her step away, and disappear inside the house. He looked around, inhaled the warm summer air, smiled at the sight of all the wild flowers and overgrown bushes he should have cleared away by now. He didn't see how the garden would ever get done, in a way he wanted it to stay exactly as it was, he didn't want this summer to end. On the grass beside him his mobile buzzed. It was a text from his mother, telling him not to be late. He cursed silently for not switching off the thing.

'Was it Romeo?' he asked when she returned.

'Yes. He wants to come home for a weekend. The poor boy'.

'He can stay outside until I'm finished', Ciaran said, lowering his face to her thighs. 'I'm not going home', he said next. 'Let me stay with you tonight'.

'You can't stay. You know you can't'.

He started kissing her thighs. She protested for a few seconds, but there was pleasure in the sounds coming out of her, and he was encouraged to continue. He moved his lips all over her legs. He turned her over and licked the ends of her calves, behind her knees, and further up moving inside her thighs. He didn't want to stop and he listened to her gentle gasps and angled his eyes so that he could watch as she arched herself up from where she lay and he placed his hands on her hips and held her tightly as he knelt in behind her.

They were curled up together when the telephone rang for the second time that evening. 'Let it ring', he said, holding her firmly. She lay there on the blanket, sighing pleasantly. Several moments later the telephone started to ring again. One more time they ignored it. The phone went off a third and fourth time before, finally, she dragged herself away from him, skipped across the grass and disappeared inside.

'How is Romeo?' Ciaran asked when she returned, reaching for her. She resisted his advances, didn't answer his question. For a long moment she didn't say anything. She looked confused, stern even. For the first time since knowing her, Ciaran felt he should say something into the silence, but he didn't know what to say. Then she looked into his eyes.

'It wasn't Romeo'.

'Oh. Who was it? Your husband?'

'Your mother. It was your mother', she said, turning away from him. 'You have to go now'.

'Will I come tomorrow?'

'No'.

He reached out an arm and tried to drag her to him. She stepped back, and pointed towards the house. 'Please', she said, not looking at him.

'What else do you want me to do?' he asked her, when they were both standing at the front door. 'Tell me. I'll do anything you want. Anything, just show me'.

She reached out to him and held his face between her hands. She had a wild look, he thought she was going to crush him, in a way he wanted her to. For a moment she clutched him tightly to her, against the silky material of the dressing gown she had put on, and gently stroked his hair. Then she placed her hands on his shoulders.

'Go and live your life', she said. There was pleading in her voice. Her eyes watered. 'Are you listening to me?'

Again, he shook his head.

'We can't see each other anymore', she said, louder again, staring intensely at him.

He leaned over and tried to kiss her. She turned her face away. Then stepped back, when he tried to close his arms around her. 'No', she shouted, dragging him to his feet as he knelt down and parted the dressing gown.

Ciaran didn't understand what was happening. She held the door as he backed away. He got on his bike and looked back one more time. The front door was closed. He pedalled slowly through the open driveway. *We can't see each other anymore.* He had no idea why she'd said that. Her husband was out of the way. He could handle his mother, give her a story. He pedalled harder now, and the harder he pedalled the less he understood. Already, he was reliving his time with Audrey but, somehow, it was getting mixed up with moments from Fiona's short life. In the distance he could see the city lights and he thought of all the questions to come from his mother, of the emptiness that lay ahead of him. Again, he thought of Fiona. And he thought of Audrey, and her flesh and her thighs. Rounding the bend he drifted over to the other side. He stared into the beams of the oncoming vehicle and pedalled wild-eyed towards them.

GUTTED

Shoved the blade of my knife in front of Anthony Kane's face. Soon as I did was yanked out of my chair and marched as far as Flood's office. He gave me the long hard stare he is famous for among ten-year-olds around here, then wanted to know what I was doing with a knife at school. Going to stab all the students and teachers was about to say, but, by then, Ma and Da had appeared and more questions were being launched in my direction. How long was I in possession of the knife? Where had it come from? Why had I felt the need to take it into school? The questions landed quickly and mostly from Ma, and there was no time to supply an answer before another one arrived. At some point, Anthony Kane was called into Flood's office to give his version of events. To listen to him you'd think I was an axe murderer. Was on the verge of saying it too, especially when Kane started waving his arms as part of his reconstruction of what had happened. Then I was asked to respond to Kane's testimony. This office is too small for so many people was all I could muster up.

The knife was a gift from Martin, my older brother. Gave it to me for my tenth birthday a week before he left for America. San Francisco he's gone to, night before he left told me he's never coming home. Was curious to see what would happen if I waved the knife at Kane and his sidekick, Gerard Duggan. Would they back off, leave me alone once and for all? Would it make them worse?

They've been at me since the beginning of the school year. Every day they wait for me to appear at the old bridge. Every day I oblige. Putting up no resistance as they get stuck in with their punches. My unwillingness to fight back, my reluctance to defend myself against their attacks has encouraged them no end. In the school yard they come and find me, taunt me at every opportunity, mock my quiet ways. Hey, Dummy, what's it like on your planet? Hey, Dummy, guess what's going to happen to you later? Hey, Dummy, where's big brother when you want him? Until I produced the knife didn't as much as flinch at what was said or done to me. They are cruel and I suppose I am an easy target for their catcalling. That is all there is to it. And so on my way home, when they emerge from where they are waiting for me, I take their abuse and the beatings they give me. Become adept at concealing my wounds.

Didn't miss Martin at first. We never spent much time together; there is the age difference; figured there'd be plenty of opportunities for us to hang out. Now he is gone, and I suppose I notice his absence more and more, miss his voice about the place, his larger presence.

Once Martin was safely landed in San Francisco Ma wasted little time. She made sure she had all his contact information. His mobile phone number. His email address. The address of the hostel he was temporarily staying in. She bought a computer. Took a beginner's computer class so that she could find out how to set up her own email address. She became an expert on Skype, and when he moved out of the hostel, made sure Martin sent on his new postal address.

Once she is ready, with every piece of information lined up beside her, she sits up late on Friday night in front of the computer screen waiting for Martin's Skype-ID button to turn green. When the expected call doesn't come through, she spends the entire night lying awake in her bed and the following day talking her way through a lengthy list of disasters that explains why Martin hasn't telephoned. He has fallen victim to an act of unprovoked violence. He has been left bleeding in the street. As she speaks the very words his injuries are going untended in a hospital emergency room. Terrorists have it in for that place, she says pointing to a map of America in the atlas she keeps near her at all times. Martin is on the west coast of America, there's bound to be an earthquake, she decided after flicking through National Geographic images of a recent disaster in Mexico. Doesn't matter what Da says to calm her worries. At any moment something bad is about to happen. 'My poor boy', is her grim-reaper conclusion, and with either hand she takes a hold of the edges of the computer table and sighs heavily.

A couple of Friday evenings after flashing the knife – once Ma had finally dragged herself away from it – sat up at the computer and tapped out an email to my brother.

Hello Bro, hope you're OK over there in San Francisco. We all miss you here and I'd have loved it if you were around to see me in action with Anthony Kane and Gerard Duggan. They picked on the wrong person one time too many when they decided to jump me in the school yard a few days ago. You should have seen them cower when I flashed the knife in their direction. Kane made a song and dance about me shoving it in his puny face and they all believed him. After that they took the knife off me. Not to worry, I'll get it back if it's the last thing I do. Enda.

PS I've been hearing about all the horrendous experiences in store for you in America. Violent assaults, terrorism, and an earthquake. Still, I think you were right to take off.

The following day – Saturday, my favourite day – went exploring the downtown streets, wandered through the Market Square. The place was buzzing with activity. Stalls selling hats, candles, cheese, mirrors, beads, belts, necklaces, finger rings and other things laid out in attractive ways. Stalls selling quickly prepared foods; curry cups, vegetable wraps and meat kebabs cut from great hunks of slowly rotating flesh. People browsed the stalls and, in their attempts to attract buyers, hawkers called out special prices. A woman on a stool looked into the future and sighed. The three-card-trick man won every game he played. With his guitar Goodtime Ray sang the down-and-out blues. In no time was dizzy from taking it all in.

At the end of the food stalls the smell of raw fish hit me. Saw a work bench, bloodstained and splattered with bits of fish scale and other discarded fish parts. Approached the bench, saw some fish nestled among iced-up trays. Was just in time to see the fishmonger bring his cleaver down on a fish head which was then tossed into a bucket. Watched as the fishmonger sliced open the fish, removed its guts and added them to the accumulating mess.

'Hello, little man. Something catch your eye', the fishmonger said to me with a hearty kind of chuckle, without looking up from his work. 'Eh. What's that you say? A fillet of haddock? Coming right up'.

Watched him gut a piece of white fish, dress it with some herbs and crumbs, wrap it in a piece of tinfoil and present it to me.

'There you go, little man. Bring that home to your mother, tell her to bung it in the oven for twenty minutes and I guarantee you she'll let you stay up to watch *Match of the Day*'.

Without a word, took the parcel and moved quickly away.

Don't speak much anymore. Nobody listens. Principal Flood with his dagger look. Da reading his paper after a day packing Tupperware in the factory. Ma in an everlasting flap about Martin. Sometimes, I hear them discuss my solitary nature, say how I should be mixing more, making friends. Me, I have my ways to discover the world. Through activities and people I see, sounds heard. Like walking on my own, presenting myself at the edge of things, have no need for language. Come Saturday, I invent the place I have to be so I can get among the streets, be in motion.

Loitered among the stalls until trade started to fall off, and traders started to pack up their wares, dismantle their stalls. Stood and watched them roll up canopies and separate metal poles which dropped to the ground with a loud clang. Watched as some traders counted their day's takings and gave out long satisfied whistles. Listened as others sighed at the paltry sums in their hands and, with a shoulder shrug or comforting back slap, took themselves as far as the pub on the square.

Was almost home when I spotted Anthony Kane and Gerard Duggan. Sitting together on the low wall that curls away from the old broken bridge. As I drew near them, they spotted me and stood up off the wall.

'Look who it is', Kane said, spreading himself all over the path.

'It's Dummy', said Duggan, joining Kane. 'The dummy who thinks he's so special'.

'Hello Dummy', said Kane. 'Where you been?'

'And what makes you so special? Go on, tell us'.

'You better tell us. Otherwise something nasty is going to happen'.

'Guess what's going to happen, Dummy?'

'We'll knock your head off the wall'.

'We'll knock your head off *every* wall'.

'Or maybe we'll rip it clean off?'

'Maybe we'll rip out your tongue? Not as if you use it. Is it, Dummy?'

Looked at the pair of them, smiling almost. Was going to say something, maybe threaten them with a new knife I suddenly thought of pretending I had, this time let them know was going to slice open one of them. Instead, tried to continue on my way, ignore their catcalls.

'Not so fast, Dummy', Kane said. 'What's in your pocket?'

Instinctively, I felt for the fish parcel.

'Empty your pockets, Dummy', said Duggan.

'On second thoughts', Kane said and pinned me to the wall as Duggan reached in my pocket and pulled out the tinfoil lump. Tried to grab it, but Duggan twisted my arm and tripped me to the ground. Kane unravelled the foil and winced as he beheld the flabby piece of fish.

'Pughh! What have we here?'

He straddled me where I lay on the path, dangled the piece of fish over me. Crumbs and herbs dropped onto my face. Closer and closer Kane leaned until the flesh was touching the tip of my nose.

'Open wide, Dummy', Kane said, but I kept my mouth shut. Kane pressed the fish against my mouth and started rubbing it over my face. It started to break apart and bits of the slippery flesh went in my eyes, up my nose, matted in my hair. Round and around my face Kane continued to rub until the piece of fish had dissolved into nothing more than a mushy goo. By the time he was finished Kane's hands were a sticky mess. He wiped them in my clothes.

'Let's go', Kane said to his sidekick. Then the pair of them took off.

Kick me hard. Throw a punch in my queasy gut. Nail me to a cross and later jab my insides with a long spear. Don't mind any of that. Can take it. It's the catcalling I'm suddenly fed up with. Jokers messing with my head all the time. Throw in a person who is not listening if I speak up and it is a bad recipe. Makes me wish I had more than a knife in my pocket. Makes me wish I was evil.

When I got home Ma was sitting at the computer. She had her hands to her face and she was shaking.

'My poor boy', she announced as I paused at the door. 'My poor, poor boy'.

She was staring at images on the computer screen, holding her hands to her head, gasping at every second of footage of some unfolding disaster. Stood at the door watching her, saw the destructive images over her shoulder, buildings collapsing, distraught faces. Stepped inside and closed the door quietly behind me. Moved towards Ma, feeling my face and running my hands through my sticky hair. Ma turned around, stared at me for a moment. Followed her gaze and looked down at the fish stains on my trousers.

Later, after I had made it to the bathroom to clean myself, and was lying on my bed, listened to Da try to calm Ma down about the hurricane; he patiently explained to her how unlikely it was that a hurricane in Alabama would harm Martin and that she should not be upsetting herself so much. There was some more talk about Martin. Then I heard my own name.

'Is he punishing us for something?' Ma said.

'He doesn't speak to anyone, Olive. He can't have it in for everyone, can he?'

'I wish Martin was here. He would know what to do. He would get him out of his shell'.

Later again, when the computer became available, tapped out another email to my brother.

Hello Bro, we all still miss you here and I hope San Francisco is treating you well and that you've been to visit Alcatraz and the Golden Gate Bridge. I was at the market earlier today myself. The fishmonger gave me some haddock, wrapped it up especially for me with herbs and stuff, said Ma would enjoy cooking it. I was on my way home with it when Kane and Duggan tried to jump me again. As I mentioned I don't have the knife any more, so I took the fish out of my pocket and used it to batter them into the middle of next week. You should have heard them squeal for mercy. I can safely say they won't be troubling me again, so there's no need to worry. Enda.

PS Mother reckons there's a hurricane heading for your front door. So watch out for that.

'My poor boy', Ma was saying first thing next morning. She was watching more images of the hurricane, roofless houses, wreckage everywhere, drowning streets. People were canoeing down the road they lived in. Rescue teams were airlifting people stranded on floating islands of rubbish. Others stood distraught among the mangled remains of what they had once called home. Then there was an image of a coastline being battered by an incredible thunderstorm. Cars took to the air. Pylons became deadly weapons. Treacherous cables started fires.

'Oh my God! Bob is in Louisiana', Ma said.

'Who is Bob?' Da asked, looking up from his paper.

'Bob is the hurricane. He is moving west. He's heading straight for Martin. I'm not going to sleep tonight. I know I won't. I think I'll take two sleeping pills'.

Allowed Kane and Duggan do their worst after school, just lay on the ground as they kicked my head and ribs, offered no resistance when they threw clenched fists into my face. Tried not to hear the names they were calling me; my only wish was that I still had the knife Flood had confiscated.

Hobbled home, preparing my stories in case I was asked about the bruising. Have started playing rugby. Fell while climbing onto the flat-roof shed in the back garden. Took one step too many along the broken bridge.

At home, Ma was busy fretting about Bob. Bill Houlihan, the cycling postman, heard all about him over slow cups of tea. Mary McDermott from next door got an earful. A cousin in London. She was still at it by the time Da got in from packing at the Tupperware factory. Bob was the only thing she wanted to talk about, what it was going to do once it arrived in Martin's back garden. Throughout the evening, Da sat patiently in his chair with his paper, occasionally twisting himself around as though it might help all the hurricane-chatter swirl away from him. He's gone and if he has any sense he won't come home, I could feel Da wanting to say to her. But he didn't.

Hello Bro, and how are you and how is San Francisco? Bill Houlihan was by today with your postcard and Ma nearly strangled him with the hug she gave him. Mind you, it didn't stop her going on about the hurricane. Apparently, it's now in Louisiana. Did I tell you it has a name – Bob. You'd swear it was a long lost relative returned to live with us the way Ma goes on about it. It's not the earthquake she was looking for, but Bob seems to be suiting her just fine. So watch out, bro, Bob is coming to get you. Ma won't be through fretting until he does. Enda.

PS Kane and Duggan are squirming in their boots every time I appear on the same path as them. And though I'm sorry they took it off me, especially it being a present from you, I may not be needing the knife after all.

'Oh my God!' Ma announced on Saturday morning, throwing her arms into the air in front of the computer screen. 'Bob has arrived in Texas. It's going to be a disaster. I know it is. My poor boy'.

'Martin isn't in Texas, he's in San Francisco', Da said, rustling his paper.

'Have you not been listening to the reports? Bob is heading that way. He is going to wipe out everything. The Sky News reporter says so and he always knows what he's talking about'.

'Are you sure about that?' Da said.

'Of course, I'm sure. Anyway, I've been reading about hurricanes – on Wikipedia. Did you know they are all given a name? Andrew. Isobel. Jerry. Katrina. Lester. Thelma. They have to alternate the names because in 1979 feminists objected to all hurricanes being named after women. And they go alphabetically, starting all over again with the letter A at the beginning of a new year. So Bob is only the second hurricane this year. Which means there are lots more to come. One year they got as far as Wendy. That's twenty-three hurricanes. Twenty-three! My poor boy'.

'Come on', Da said, tapping me on the shoulder.

Winced. Usually, Da had a lie-in on Saturday after his week's work. Meant I was almost always up and out and disappeared before Da had a chance to suggest doing something together. Not this Saturday. Da was up, had eaten breakfast, endured Ma's daily dose and was as eager as me to hit the streets.

Once downtown, among the familiar streets and side alleys, it was easy giving him the slip. Headed for the Market Square as soon as I knew I was alone. Arrived at the fish stall. Looked on as the fishmonger slid his knife along the fish, removed the guts and tossed them in the bucket. Watched some more as he filleted a piece of fish, dressed it with some chillies and garlic and herbs, then wrapped it inside a piece of tinfoil. Other onlookers had stopped to watch, and listened to the fishmonger enthusiastically relay the benefits of fish and how easy it is to cook, how not so tough on the wallet it is. After the little speech, one or two onlookers purchased some of the tinfoil wraps set aside. While these transactions took place, stepped closer to the fishmonger's work bench, took a long look at the implements laid out in front of him.

'Can I help you there, little man?' the fishmonger called over. He was wrapping another piece of fish for a customer, like before not looking directly at me, though aware of my presence, as money and fish exchanged hands.

'Tell us, did she let you watch *Match of the Day?*' the fishmonger asked next. By now, he was looking straight at me.

Shook my head and stepped away. Walked the line of food stalls, moved further inside the market, among the busier stalls. Was surrounded by people, shuffling through the narrow passageways, jostling for the best way through, all the time chattering incessantly, could hardly make out a word that was said. At some point spotted Da trying on a hat. Ducked down another aisle. Then saw Anthony Kane. For once, he wasn't with his sidekick. He was with his Ma and Philip, his smaller brother. They were at a scarf and gloves stall, and Kane's Ma was trying to get her older son to try on some gloves. Kane was squirming as his Ma wrestled a pair of mittens around his hands.

At some point, Kane saw me looking his way and flashed me a look that said *just you wait*. Didn't turn away. Instead, watched my classmate struggle to drag himself free from his Ma's fussing. Kane was shaking his head wildly and his Ma was having to use up all her energy keeping him still. During their struggle the smaller boy, Philip, wandered over to me.

'What did you put in your pocket?' Philip asked me, sounded just like his older brother. Pretended not to have heard the question. Inside my pocket allowed my fingers touch the sharp edge of the fish knife I had taken, looked down at Philip.

'I saw you take something from the bench', Philip tried again. 'What have you got?'

'A fish. I have a fish in my pocket'.

'Show me. I want to see it'.

Kept looking down at the boy. He was tiny, little more than a pip.

'OK. But not here. We have to go somewhere'.

'Go where?'

Took Philip by the hand and led him away from the stalls, away from the market place. Wasn't sure yet where I was taking him, maybe we could do a little exploring together, see if there was anything interesting happening on the streets, down one of the alleys. Maybe we could head as far as the old broken bridge. As we moved through the crowd, Philip looked up at me, his little face an expression of wonder, his busy mouth opening and closing. Just like a fish, it occurred to me as I led the boy further and further away.

The Fortune Teller and the Rebel

I was once friends with a lady who could see into the future. Everyone called her Gypsy Teresa, but I knew her by her real name – Cassie. Cassie wasn't like other fortune tellers. She didn't insist you drink a cup of tea and then peer into the empty cup for an examination of the way the tea-leaves arranged themselves. She didn't have a crystal ball or use magic cards. She didn't follow the lines on your hand and tell you what mazy patterns signified. She just spent her days at the low-end of the lane that ran along the ends of the houses, staring into the ditchwater. If people wanted to hear what she had to say they knew where to find her.

Every day, upon returning from my expedition downtown, I passed her in the back lane.

'Hello Cassie', I'd say. 'Tell me, where am I going to be in ten years time?'

I waited for a reply, but none came.

'OK. We'll leave it at five years. Where will I be in five years, Cassie?'

Still nothing.

'OK so. Let's bring it back to one year. Where will I be in a year's time, Cassie?'

Still nothing.

'Tell you what, Cassie. Keep it to yourself for now. Tell me next time. OK'.

And I continued on my way.

In our town fortune telling was quickly becoming a clever career move. Just about everybody on our road, for instance, was curious about the future. They had to know what was going to happen. Who is the person most likely to be a thorn in everyone's side? When is my annoying mother-in-law going to kick the bucket? What are tonight's Lotto numbers? No question was too outrageous.

There were two other big differences between Cassie and other fortune tellers. The first was that Cassie didn't charge for letting people know what was in store for them. The second was that she had no qualms about handing out bad news. Choosing Cassie's services over any of the others brought out the gambler in a person.

Some heard everything they wanted to and more. 'You're going to live to be a hundred', she told Kitty Forbes. 'You will see Sydney Harbour', she said to Patsy Regan. 'You will own a wonderful collection of shoes', she told Maura Kelly. Others were not so lucky.

At night, I discussed the future with my sister, Ciara. Since turning fifteen Ciara had been the rebel in our house. She was four years older than me and had a sudden plan she wanted me to listen to. Before she started into her plan she gave me her little speech. She had composed the speech some time back and it always helped put her in the right mood for what it was she really wanted to talk about.

'I'm sick of everything', she began on this occasion. 'I'm sick of this bog-hole town. Sick of the useless road we live on. Sick of the house we live in. I'm sick of everyone in our town. Sick of everyone on this useless road. Sick of Ma. I even get sick of you sometimes. Everything makes me sick'.

'OK', I said.

'Well, aren't you going to ask me what I intend to do about it?'

'What do you intend to do about it?'

'I'm running away. And this time I mean it. At this point you should be getting interested in finding out when I'm planning to be off'.

'When are you off?'

'Friday'.

'Today is Tuesday'.

'Why are you so interested in days of the week all of a sudden? You should be trying to find out where I'm planning to go'.

'Where will you go?'

'I can't tell you. Otherwise I'll have to kill you'.

'OK'.

Talking with Ciara about the future wasn't much fun. Talking to her about anything else wasn't fun either. It was a pity I was related to her. But that was my lot.

Days were long and full of possibilities. I thought everything was ahead of me, was curious about the world, wondered at the immensity of it. I also wanted a head start, needed to know things before I had a chance to experience them first hand, and so I thought it clever to seek out the services of one of the town's visionaries. Because I had no money I chose Cassie over the others. Besides, I didn't like the taste of tea, was afraid of the crystal ball. The idea of a wizened old lady grabbing my hands and then shuddering didn't appeal to me at all.

Because it was a time of few prospects and people didn't have as much money as they used to, many decided to throw caution to the wind and take their chances with Cassie. They were prepared to risk receiving a little bad news if it meant not having to pay. And, who knows, it might be good news Cassie had for them – it was worth the gamble, everyone felt. And anyway, things could not get any worse than they now were.

And so the next time I passed along the back lane I had to join a line of people waiting to speak with Cassie. Spit McLoughlin was in front of me, coughing and spluttering. I asked him what he wanted with Cassie and he looked suspiciously at me.

'Why do you ask?' he said, in that musical way he had of talking.

'No reason, Spit. I just wanted to pass time while we wait'.

'Did I ask you what you want with her?'

'No'.

'Mind your own feckin' business then'.

As soon as he spat a gob-full of phlegm onto the ground, I turned away from Spit and saw The Slug Doyle. I was about to ask him the same question I had asked Spit, but he beat me to it.

'What are you here for, Little Man?'

'Ciara is pulling a disappearing act on Friday', I said. 'I want to find out where she's headed'.

The Slug let out a long shrill whistle at this. Then he waved me close to him.

'People are disappearing all the time. All you have to do is turn on the nine o'clock news. First thing they tell you is someone has disappeared. Last night I turned it on. And guess what? Two had disappeared. One in Tipperary and one in Tierra del Fuego. The other night some eejit took off in a canoe. He was last seen heading for the Atlantic. Another night some poor bastard went to post a letter. Vanished into thin air. Mind you, they found the letter. It was addressed to his Ma. Loads go missing in July. August is the worst'.

Before I had a chance to respond to The Slug there was a terrible howl up ahead of us. 'Ah jaysus!' The Slug said, standing up on his toes for a better view. 'Don't tell me George Wall is after asking about his exploration shares. I told him not to. Poor George. Poor, poor George'.

'Hello Cassie', I said when I finally joined her by the ditchwater. 'Have you any idea where my sister Ciara is planning to head for next Friday?'

She didn't say a word. She just wrapped her arms around herself and stared down into the dirty water.

'Well, do you know what she's up to today?'

She still didn't say a word.

'Well, how about telling me where she'll be in, say, a half hour's time? That'll do for now'.

Still nothing. She just stared into the ditchwater, swaying.

'Nice talking to you, Cassie', I said and continued on my way.

Ciara enjoyed trips to the bathroom mirror and the weighing scales in the kitchen. Trips to the weighing scales were usually followed by a tantrum. Then she went on hunger strike. For days she didn't eat a thing. Except maybe a cup-a-soup or a Drifter bar. She enjoyed the occasional slice of ham, but it had to be Brady's Baked Ham and that wasn't always easy to get. Thanks to previous hunger strikes she was now so skinny that if she turned sideways you wouldn't see her. If she stuck out her tongue she reminded me of a thumbtack.

On the Wednesday before Ciara was planning to run away, Ma found some Brady's Baked Ham in a shop in the neighbouring town at a bargain price, and she bought fifteen slices. When she left it in the fridge I discovered I enjoyed Brady's Baked Ham too, and made short work of our supply. 'You greedy little fucker', Ciara roared at me when she decided to call an end to her current hunger strike. 'You didn't even leave one slice'. For the next two hours she went on and on about it, about me not leaving one slice of Brady's Baked Ham. So mad was she, she wouldn't even sleep under the same roof as us that night. Instead, she marched out to Ma's putt-putt Toyota and locked herself into the car and spent the rest of the night curled up in the back seat. At some point in the night Ma threatened to throw Ciara out of the house once and for all. 'I'm already out, you witch', Ciara replied and large tears sprung from her eyes. Weighing scales and Brady's Baked Ham. These were the kinds of things that put her against the world. She was a strange rebel.

While she waited for Friday to come around Ciara spent her time in front of the television. To make herself comfortable, she dragged the floor mat back as far as the fireplace so that she could smoke up the chimney while she was flicking channels. This could take some time because the TV had more than three hundred channels thanks to Ma allowing some lad who appeared at the door one day talk her into signing up for the most expensive multi-channel deal going. I didn't know why Ciara bothered flicking because she always ended up watching the same channel – the cooking channel. She never missed *Ready Steady Cook*, *Nigella Bites*, *The Naked Chef* and *Two Fat Ladies* which was her favourite. Once she stopped flicking, she lit up her cigarette. Ma didn't like Ciara smoking in the living room because she often fell asleep with a burning cigarette in her hand. There were lots of burn marks in the yellow floor mat to prove it. Once upon a time it had been an expensive floor mat given to Ma as a birthday present from her brother Pete. By now it was full of black holes.

When I got back after my latest conversation with Cassie, Ciara was snoozing in front of a TV show featuring a kitchen of learner-cooks. A chef was teaching them. He had a funny way of doing it. 'Fuck me', he said as soon as one of his pupils put on a saucepan of potatoes. Soon the learner-cook was in tears. 'Fuck me', the chef said again, as soon as he saw the tears and the learner-cook ran out of the kitchen. 'Fuck me', he said again, flicking his apron and going wrinkly all over. If it was me, I wouldn't have run away. I'd have grabbed the saucepan and clattered Mr Fuck Me over the head. Imagine if he ever landed inside our kitchen. *Oh my, that is very delicious, the most delicious thing I have ever tasted,* he'd tell Ma, licking the fingers he had just poked into one of her simmering pots. Like hell he would. *Fuck fuck fuck fuck me,* he'd say to her when he saw what she was up to and give her several clips across the ears.

The other fortune tellers had started to feel the brunt of Cassie's free-of-charge operation. In order to attract some business the tea-leaf lady took out box-space in the current issue of the *Golden Pages.* The palm reader, card lady and crystal ball women all pasted notices in libraries, on supermarket notice boards; flyers were left on bar tables, coffee counters and placed alongside other hopeful notices at the employment centre.

Ciara had no interest in talking to Cassie or any of the other fortune tellers. She didn't want to find out what was in store for her, didn't care what would happen. That's what being a rebel is about, she said when I grilled her about it. Then she went on hunger strike again.

I didn't like it when Ciara went on hunger strike. She lost interest in everything, was tired all the time; tears rolled down her face for no reason and left dark tracks under her eyes. I didn't know what to say to her when she cried, had no idea what was so upsetting for her. I sat beside her once or twice, made her cup-a-soups, promised her all the Brady's Baked Ham I could lay my hands on. Nothing I said cheered her up.

'Are you really going tomorrow?' I asked her on the Thursday night.

'There is no turning back this time', she said.

'Is it really so bad here?'

'It's bad everywhere, brother'.

'What time are you leaving?'

'Oh, I'm in no hurry. I might have a lie in – there's no telling when I'll get another chance to snooze. I expect I'll be gone by mid-afternoon. Teatime at the latest. Before I take off, I'm going to Burger King for my last meal in this town. You can come if you want – my treat'.

'Time is running out, Cassie', I said first thing next morning. 'If you have anything to say to me, now would probably be the best time'.

She clutched herself and swayed a little. Something lurking in the muddy depths stirred some ripples in the ditchwater. Then a frog stuck his throbbing head out of the water, took a look around, decided he didn't like what he saw and ducked below again. Cassie swayed some more.

'Like I say, Cassie, I was up very early to get a good place in the queue. Everyone else gets what they want to hear. You told The Slug he is going to make Dinah Joyce a very happy woman. You told Spit McLoughlin that within five years he is going to become mayor. Everybody gets an answer from you. I think I should too'.

She swayed a little more, even moved her lips as though she wanted to say something, as though the answer to my question was there, but something inside her was preventing the words catching the light of day.

'Cassie, I am going to have to reconsider our friendship', I said, sure that my direct approach would melt the resistance inside her.

She didn't even look at me.

I met Ciara near teatime in Burger King. She was sitting in a sit-four booth when I arrived. I looked at the soggy chips on the plate in front of her, the sea of red sauce she was dipping them into.

'That's not much of a last meal', I said, sitting into the booth opposite her.

'Well, I have this', she answered, then reached into the small rucksack resting on the chair beside her, pulled out a bottle of Champagne and set it down on the plastic table.

'Let me guess. That's part of being a rebel too'.

'Got it in one, brother'.

She popped the cork under the table. At once, the Champagne spurted out and before it fizzed all over us, Ciara grabbed two paper cups and poured into each of them. She slid one of the cups towards me and raised her own. The manager spotted what we were at.

'You can't drink Champagne in here', he said when he approached our table. 'This is Burger King'.

'Spin on that', Ciara said, showing him the finger she often produced at home for Ma and me.

'I'll be back', he said, turning on his heels.

'Do you know any good toasts?' Ciara asked me next.

'To the answers', I said, raising my cup, but she didn't know what the response was. 'You're supposed to say, *to the questions*'.

Instead, she stood up out of her seat, buttoned up her denim jacket, brought the paper cup to her mouth and gulped down every drop.

'See you in the next world, brother', she said, tossing the cup, and marched to the door. Her tattered runners flapping at the ground. Her skinny legs looking like a pair of stilts that had been jammed into her backside. At the door she looked over her shoulder briefly – at what I couldn't tell – then she pulled open the door, walked away and, in times to come, no matter how often I asked, Cassie never uttered a single word to me about where she had gone.

UNTOUCHABLE

From the first moment she was the one. Her black shaggy hair. Her death-is-nigh complexion. Her lost eyes and faraway voice. She glided over ground.

He saw her every day on the bus. 'I've fallen for you', he whispered, sinking into the seat behind her.

His world was full of order, neat arrays, reconciled. She didn't know her age; forgot days of the week; paid no attention to the time of day.

'We mesh', he told himself. 'We belong together. We should meet each other halfway'.

She flung her money at the barman. 'Easy come, easy go', he heard her say. Which was all she wanted to do. Go. Hike. Climb. Sleep close to the stars. Travel along the bottom of the night. He followed every step, admiring from afar.

In the end, she said he was too clingy. He was squeezing her space.

'Have a nice life', she told him.

He hadn't even touched her.

He sent her gifts: a set of binoculars; a telescopic camera; a four-layer expedition knife. The knife had everything: a Maglite to pinpoint in dark places; a mini-saw that was easy to use; an altimeter to indicate how far off the ground she was, how close to the stars. It came all the way from Switzerland in a finger-sized pouch.

The knife was the last straw. She returned it to him with a note. *Stay away from me.* She kept the binoculars and camera.

He liked her even more when she was fiery. His loins curdled. He needed to touch her. Once.

A last warning arrived: *As much as lay a finger on me, you'll be sorry.* It gave him an idea.

The pouch arrived, flecked with gouts of red. She unsnapped it and the finger pointed at her. Like an accusation. A paper pill spilled out. And a note to explain:

I need to touch you.

The Spanish Arch Whores

I had just popped my fifth Demerol and was settling down in front of the extended version of *Apocalypse Now* when my friend Duffy called.

'Let's go and get some ice-cream, Tim', he said. 'It's been a long time'.

'Duffy, it's two o'clock in the morning', I said, but my friend wasn't interested in hearing anything like that. Life for Duffy was just one continuous now. Hours. Minutes. Seconds. Clocks. Calendars. Yesterday. Tomorrow. Next year. These were words from a language he was never going to speak.

Duffy had his own way of saying things. He spoke in code and liked to make his intentions known through a convoluted system of facial ticks, bodily gestures and unfinished sentences. To make things interesting he threw in the occasional metaphor. Take this ice-cream business. When Duffy called me up at two o'clock in the morning suggesting we go and share an ice-cream together he wasn't talking about a dark-of-night shopping trip for Choc Ices and Wibbly Wobbly Wonders. No. What Duffy meant was that he wanted to go down to the old harbour and look for whores.

Usually, I didn't mind him calling me up so late. But these pills I had been taking were slowing me down a little. I needed to slow down. I hadn't slept in the best part of a week. I had been worrying again, an activity that involved pacing tirelessly around my eight-by-twelve room, and then watching reruns of my favourite movies until my eyes took on the appearance of glazed almonds. Previously I had tried other methods. Push ups. Red wine. Endless loops of the city on my trusty bicycle. None of it had helped. Desperation had sent me to the pills and I was falling for them in a big way.

Fifteen minutes later I was on Tone Bridge waiting for Duffy. The water was high, almost flush with the pier. It was a calm night, quiet at this hour, and I could see stars watching over the old harbour.

The old harbour was my favourite part of town. Especially at night. Daytime crowds had dispersed. The pier lamps lit the way and roped-up fishing boats rested quietly while their owners sought out dark medicine. The scene comforted me and I was happy to be a part of it.

Duffy was excited – he always was whenever we met up like this. Looking for whores always turned him into a big kid.

'Tonight's the night, Tim', he said, rubbing his hands together and moving from one leg onto the other. 'I can feel it. I can feel their presence'.

'I hope you're right, Duffy', I said, smiling at my friend. 'I don't have the energy for a wild goose chase'.

I looked into his face. At once I knew he was high. His mother was a pharmacist and whenever the opportunity presented itself – which was pretty much every minute of the day – Duffy liberated pills from the cabinets of his mother's place of work. The Goldmine Duffy called it, and boy was he making the most of his claim.

'I could do with something', I said, 'a little pick-me-up', and at once he offered me a selection from the cellophane bag he took from his pocket. I popped something yellow into my mouth, something long and rectangular I had to bite into, then Duffy clapped an arm on my shoulder and we moved off the bridge in the direction of the Spanish Arch.

I had met him not long after I'd moved here. I was worrying one night and had gone for a long walk, drifted through some quiet streets, ended up in the old part of town – the part around the harbour. A corner bar tempted me – a dimly lit place with a rickety counter and even more rickety bar staff – and Duffy was on a stool making a couple of American girls laugh so much they were dribbling Guinness down their chins. The four of us stayed up drinking together, and much later, after we had managed to ditch the Americans and we were wobbling across Tone Bridge, Duffy insisted on showing me the Spanish Arch. 'Some friendly girls hang out around here', he told me, trying to wink at the same time. I let him take me to the Arch, listened to his history lesson about the thing, and tiptoed quietly behind him as he poked his head into unlit alleyways and around dark corners in search of his elusive friends. We didn't run into any whores that night, nor had we run into any along our many subsequent expeditions. I didn't mind. Duffy had a knack for calling me when I was restless. More often than not, I was happy to indulge his lusty whims.

'This is my last chance', Duffy was saying, as we stepped along the pier.

'What are you talking about?' I said.

'I have to get out of town. Lay low for a while. Vanish'.

'Problems?'

'Yeah, problems'.

'New or existing?'

'That's right'.

Duffy attracted problems the way a rabbit did snakes. Just last week we were having a meal together in an upstairs restaurant overlooking Shop Street. It wasn't the most expensive place and they served great portions. Plus, we nearly always managed to duck out without paying. I had ordered beef bourguignon and a bottle of red wine. Duffy was having a plate of Grade A oysters with his wine. For a while we had the place to ourselves. It was a Monday night, and from our window seats we could see the rain pelting down, stabbing the empty street with incessant razorous thrusts. Duffy was bored – Mondays tended to do that to him – and to amuse himself he'd started flicking on and off his Zippo lighter. At some point the curtain caught fire and the waitress threw a hissy fit. Then, of all people, Halligan walked in. Halligan was my landlord and a madman. He was also a detective sergeant. He saw the commotion with the curtain and made a move towards us. As he approached our table I wondered did he know that for the past six weeks Duffy had been pleasuring his wife. By now, Duffy had lit a cigarette and was relaxing. He glanced at the blackened curtain. He blew a circle of smoke towards Halligan. Halligan reached a hand in his pocket and produced his badge.

'What's he after showing you there, Duffy?' I asked my friend.

'His pass card', Duffy said, blowing out more circles.

Halligan picked Duffy up and threw him down the stairs of the restaurant and out onto the drenched street. He kicked him into a gulley and slapped him around for a few minutes. He left me alone because I knew about some things he was mixed up in. So I sat back into my seat and drank some more wine. A short time later, I saw Duffy standing in the street, looking up at me. He was smoking again, and looking none the worse for the beating he'd just received. He was signalling for me to join him. But it was wet out there and I hadn't finished my meal, and I liked the look of the bottle of wine Duffy had left behind, and so I let him wait for a little while longer.

'Can you see any?' he asked me, pausing near the edge of the pier.

'No', I said.

'Me neither'.

He took a couple of steps forward, until he was standing right at the edge of the pier, and staring into the black water.

'I don't think you'll see them down there', I said to my friend.

'Did you read about that boy they found?'

'I don't read, Duffy', I told him. 'It keeps me awake'.

'You should read', he said. 'It's informative'.

'What are you talking about?'

'What am I talking about? I'm talking about that boy that went off the bridge the other night'.

'What boy?'

'They found him washed up on Silver Strand. That's the fourth one this year. And it's only February. The fourth. Think of it'.

'I don't want to think, Duffy. Thinking keeps me awake, and gets me hot and bothered. Now can we talk about something else?'

'All I'm saying is that I don't like reading about these boys. There has to be a way to save them. Not have them jumping off bridges. I'm going to take something. Need anything?'

'Yes I do, but don't give me another yellow – it was really bitter'.

'Here's a blue. It's chalky – try it'.

Then there was the matter of his looks. Duffy looked exactly like James Dean – I mean exactly the way the doomed actor looked in *Rebel Without a Cause*. Sometimes, to rub in the effect, he brushed back his hair and wore a waist-length red canvas jacket – with the collar turned up. You could see the women in Naughtons quivering when he put a cigarette in his mouth and let it dangle. Some of the lads in there quivered too. At first this wasn't a problem. Duffy enjoyed all the attention. Especially from the ladies. Inside Naughtons they climbed over each other to get within touching distance of his long eyelashes and red sleeves. They liked his impish smile and the hint of teeth that came with it. He had good teeth, Duffy. He looked after them. Problems started, however, when Duffy got into a persistent habit of booking himself on long romantic nights in the company of married women.

'Why do they have to be married?' I asked him one night.

'Talk to them, not me', he said.

'I worry for you, Duffy', I said.

'There are better things in this world to worry about', he said.

'Maybe, but this world isn't kind to people like you'.

'The world, the world', he said. 'Let me tell you what I think of the world'.

'OK'.

'The world is a bed'.

'Is that a metaphor?' I asked next and he shrugged his shoulders.

And so, as we stepped towards the Arch and the temperature started to go down and fog started to roll in, Duffy began telling me about his immediate problems. In total there were five. Their names were Vanessa, Siobhan, Miriam, Zadie and The Witch. Three of these problems were closely related. He told me he found it difficult to tell Vanessa and Siobhan apart. Minutes separated them at birth, and, the other night, when he'd gasped *fortissimo Siobhan*, Vanessa's fingernails carved into his cantering buttocks an intricate network of trenches. Miriam was similarly clingy, he said, and wanted whatever it was her older sisters had.

'Jesus!' I said, thinking of some long fingernails I'd seen not long before. 'That must have been sore'.

'It was worth it', he said.

Were it not for her unsurpassable shape he said he would with pleasure dropkick Zadie into the bay. The Witch was the only one of them he could stomach for more than a day. With her, boredom was not an issue because, at a moment's notice, she could become anything he desired. Until recently they were unaware of the bit part they each played in his life. This, he felt, absolved him of doing the right thing. A man with a variety of needs was how he described himself. I was lost in admiration for his facility for understatement.

'And they're all married?' I said to him.

'Let me see. Siobhan is. Vanessa is. Miriam has a boyfriend. I've met him. They're getting married soon'.

'What about Zadie?'

'Oh yes, she's married to a big broth of a lad with five brothers. Two of them are kickboxers. They've successfully represented the province at the national kickboxing championships'.

'Is that last bit a metaphor?'

'No'.

'Duffy, explain to me again why we need to look for whores'.

'Not everything can be explained', he said.

When we reached the Arch the fog was thickening. It was still calm. The water was a scarcely billowing black cloak. I could still make out the resting boats.

A drunk was laid out on the cobblestones beneath the Arch. He looked like something Forthill Cemetery had spat out. He had the largest ears I had ever seen. He was sleeping and, for a moment, I almost envied him.

'Look', Duffy said, pointing him out to me.

'Yes, I see', I said.

'This is good', Duffy said. 'This lad will tell us what we need to know'.

'He's asleep, Duffy', I said.

With the heel of his shoe Duffy nudged the drunk who jolted violently into life.

'Not any more', Duffy said.

The drunk spun himself into a sitting position, and leaned back against the glistening stone of the Arch. Duffy reached inside his pocket, and fetched out a tenner.

'We need some information', he said, waving the tenner in front of the drunk.

'Information!' the drunk cackled.

'That's right', Duffy said, waving the money note closer and closer to the drunk. 'If you can give me the information I want I'll give you this'.

'Make it a twenty and you have a deal', said the drunk.

Duffy backed up and, for a minute, I thought he was going to leave it at that. But I knew he was enjoying this little pantomime with the rag-and-bone apparition in front of us, and he fetched out of his pocket a couple of more notes.

'OK. Any sign of the whores?' Duffy asked him, handing over the first tenner.

'I saw one standing right where you are now', the drunk replied, stuffing the money note inside his tattered coat.

'How did you know she was a whore?' Duffy asked, brandishing a second tenner.

'Because when I offered her the money the last pair of clowns gave me she hitched her skirt and hooked her legs behind my ears'.

'How long ago was this?' Duffy asked, passing over a third tenner.

'About fifty years ago'.

'Give me back my money', Duffy said, but it was too late for refunds. The drunk had sprung to his feet and had legged it, yahooing into the quickly cooling night.

'Look at him go', Duffy said.

'He's a quick one', I agreed.

We stepped beyond the Arch and out along the Long Walk. The houses facing the water loomed tall. It was late and every light was out. People were in bed. The fog was thickening further, the dews pricked my skin and, ahead of us, the pier lights became fuzzy blurs. I was starting to think of what Duffy had said about the world being a bed. It made me want to lie down.

'Can you see any?'

'No'.

'Neither can I. Can you see anything?'

I scanned all around me, so as to have something to say. As soon as I gazed towards the water, a fleet of swans materialized through the fog. One by one they appeared, and they floated gracefully past me in single file, in the direction of the bridge.

'Well?' Duffy said into the silence. 'What do you see?'

'I can see swans', I said.

'Swans!'

'Yep. Swans'.

'I can't see any swans. How many can you see?'

'I don't know. Thirty-five. Maybe fifty'.

'Come on, let's try down this alley'.

I followed Duffy down an open alleyway offering access to an old courtyard. We met nobody in the alleyway. The courtyard was quiet. Ivy covered the stone walls surrounding us. Wisps of fog hovered over the cobblestones. Somewhere a dog barked.

'When are you leaving, Duffy?' I asked him.

'Tomorrow'.

'Tomorrow! That's short notice. How is your mother about all of this?'

'The mother is delighted. She's had enough of my aimless ways. She's ordered me to spend some time with a relation somewhere in arctic Canada. Some madman who shoots geese and dances with bears. She's even gone and bought me a flight ticket. But I think I'll go to Italy'.

'Italy! I've always wanted to go there. Which part?'

'I know a girl from Bologna. She has fantastic hands'.

'Do they come with fingernails?'

We retraced our steps. I looked around, hoping to see the swans again, but the fog was swirling around us now and it was becoming increasingly difficult to see. I sighed into the gathering whiteness, my foggy breath giving birth to shapes I had never seen.

'Look at that, Duffy', I said, breathing out and then pointing to the wispy patterns floating before me.

Duffy looked at me, raised his arms and let them fall back to his sides again.

'I don't know, Tim', he said, wandering out ahead of me. 'This place used to teem with whores'.

'That's right', I said, through the whiteness he had vanished into. 'About fifty years ago. Be careful', I said next. 'It drops off somewhere around here'. But I didn't think he was listening.

'Where could they be?' was all I heard him say as he disappeared further inside the accumulating fog.

I strained to see how far ahead of me he had drifted. I wouldn't see him again after tonight, not for a long time. I wanted him to find these women.

Next thing I started to see ripples of dancing light. Streaks of fluorescent green waving like curtains. The light was mingling with the fog in rapid vibrating bursts, making wavy patterns, and flashing hither and thither through the fog, glowing luminously as it moved.

'Can you see it, Duffy?' I called out to my friend. 'My word it's beautiful. Please tell me you can see it. Duffy, where are you?' I called out.

For a moment there was nothing from my friend. Nothing except a great silence and this dancing light.

Then I heard him.

'I can see it. Jesus Christ! Tim, I can see it. Do you realise what this is?'

'I realise those chalky blue pills are worth their weight in gold. Have you any more?'

'No, no, no. It's not the pills. It's the aurora borealis'.

'What's that, Duffy?'

'The aurora borealis. We are looking at the aurora borealis. My mother said I would see it when I got to Canada'.

'We're not in Canada, Duffy. We're somewhere near the end of the Long Walk'.

'Man, it's beautiful. Get over here, Tim. You can see more'.

'Be careful, Duffy', I called out again.

The fog was all around me now. From previous trips I knew there was no barrier at the end of the pier. Duffy was somewhere out in front of me but everything had become a vast snowy haze. The fog was in constant motion, swirling around me, I could taste the glints of moisture from it. I was tired, a little dizzy and I sat down. As soon as I did I could hear music. It was vague, at first, something distant and indecipherable. Gradually, though, I started to make some sense of it. A boys' choir performing a hymn from a Latin Mass, the voices at once angelic and haunting.

'Duffy', I called out. 'Can you hear that? I think it's coming from the sky. Something tells me we're not going to find anyone out here tonight'.

He didn't reply. Nor could I see him. And all I could hear were the harmonies of this beautiful hymn reaching deep inside me. I lay down on the cold ground and closed my eyes. I could have listened to it forever. I checked my pockets for more pills, but there was nothing there.

'Duffy', I tried again. 'I wouldn't say no to another pill'.

There was no reply. The fog was wrapping itself further and further around me. I thought about standing up and making a tentative move back in the direction we had come from. But I was no longer certain of where to place my feet, and so I stayed put and lay rigidly where I was. Then I started to worry.

It was at that precise moment I heard the panting behind me, fast steps along the ground. At first, I thought it was my friend, that he had somehow double-backed on me and was now doing his best to spook me. I still couldn't make out a thing in the fog. The panting increased, the movement hastened and, sitting up, I quietly cursed my friend. Then the moving form exploded through the fog. It wasn't Duffy. It was a girl. Most likely I only saw her for a fraction of a second but the pills I'd taken had slowed everything down and from where I was sitting already it seemed to me that I had been looking at her for an eternity. She couldn't have been more than seventeen. She had black lustrous hair falling below her shoulders. Her skin was pale. Her eyes glistened. She had a lead weight tied around her neck. She blitzed past me and disappeared into the whiteness ahead. She didn't look at me, didn't register my presence, didn't break her stride. A moment later I heard a splash.

'Jesus Christ!' somebody yelled. It was Duffy. 'Jesus Christ!' he called out again. And again. 'Jesus Christ!'

I stood up and moved forward, towards what I assumed was the pier-end. With every step I doubted myself further. I knew it must be close, but still I could make out nothing. Then I heard a second splash. I quickened my pace. Heard someone thrashing about in the water below. I reached the end of the pier.

'Duffy', I whispered. 'Is that you?'

'Can you see her?' he called up to me. 'She's in the water. Can you see?'

I couldn't see a thing. I knelt down, then lay down so that my head reached out over the lip of the pier. I didn't know what to expect. I rolled over on my back and, once again, I was looking at the light-show performing for me. It was a ragged performance, luminous and shambolic – the dance of some agitated nocturnal spirit. Then I could hear Duffy kicking about in the water, gasping for air, for a sign from me. I no longer knew what was happening.

'What's going on?' I called down to him as quietly as I could.

'What are you whispering for? We've got to save this girl. Do you hear me?'

Suddenly he was screeching, a man possessed by some crazy purpose. I could hear him thrashing around in the water and taking heavy gulps of air and calling out for the missing girl. Something momentous was happening. I could feel it fizzing through my body, reaching every fibre within me. 'We've got to save her', I heard my friend say again. I stood back up and looked around me. I was engulfed by a thick soupy fog. I closed my eyes as though it was a way out of there, and, while I stood there, I heard a chorus of angels pleading with me to take the wreckage that was my life and put it back together again. When I opened my eyes I knew I wasn't going anywhere. I took a couple of steps back, and stared up at the flickering green light. I smiled briefly, peered into the swirling white abyss in front of me and dove in.

Alan McMonagle was born in Sligo, grew up in Longford and now lives in Galway. He has received awards for his work from the Professional Artists' Retreat in Yaddo (New York), the Fundación Valparaiso (Spain), the Banff Centre for Creativity (Canada) and The Arts Council (Ireland). His stories have appeared in many journals in Ireland and North America including *The Adirondack Review*, *The Valparaiso Fiction Review*, *Natural Bridge*, *Grain*, *Prairie Fire*, *Southword* and *The Stinging Fly*. *Liar Liar* (Wordsonthestreet), his first collection of stories appeared in 2008 and was longlisted for the Frank O'Connor International Short Story Award in 2009. The title story of this new collection, *Psychotic Episodes,* was nominated for a 2011 Pushcart Prize.